Published by DTstories

# Contents:

## Introduction

## By The Treasure Troll

I likes stories, I do. I tracks them down and steals them, wherever I can find them, and I bring them back here to my cave. My story trove. I keep my stories here and I read them. Sometimes I read them to the faeries — it's the only thing that keeps the pesky things quiet.

I steals all kinds of stories. Long stories and short stories. Happy stories and sad stories. Scary stories and funny stories. Stories about love and stories about fighting. I steals them all and brings them back to my story trove.

Then I finded a really great trove of stories at a place called Rye House, where Sean, Sandra, Sue and Nyki started going to read their stories out. David and Lynette came later, too, but then they got tricksy and all disappeared. Perhaps they suspected me.

I tracked them down at last, though, I did, to a place called The Six Templars in Hertford. The ale there's as good as any inn where adventurers meet in secret, and I steals that as well as their stories. And I tracked Sandra down later to a far-off kingdom called Chichester. I steals her stories from there.

There's stories in my trove set in this world, and other worlds, and even no worlds at all. There's stories that's really exciting, and some that make me laugh and some that make me cry. The faeries cry, too, but not at the right stories. Silly things. There's even stories that don't have no story at all, and has all their lines cut up. I think them stories are called pomes or something.

So I'm going to share all my story trove with you, I am. Just come inside my cave, so you can listen. Come on, I isn't going to eat you.

Well, not much.

# The Festival of Nets

## Part One: Bone Charms

## By Sean Patrick Giblin

Demen's first easy step into Salt Breeze, the illustrious lower city of the grand capital of Al'Cier, was one of grim joy. Above the cobbled streets hung a decorative display of the previous night's revelry; he smirked beneath his charcoal travel-grown beard. Feet danced in the wind, and the creaking of the swinging nooses from above was drowned out only by the cacophony of the crowd mixing beneath the ghastly banners. He saw none of the city's famed, Thief Catchers, whose work now so proudly adorned the upper ramparts of the Quarter's four storey tenements. After all the Festival of Nets was as much their night as it was his and his kind's.

It was an auspicious time of year, when the two moons, the Fisher, the patron of thieves and the Watcher, lord of judgement and justice, crossed paths in the night sky. The Fisher was nothing more than a thin sickle of green opulent light in the late evening sky, a good omen among thieves. The Watcher, in all its dark glory, hung full as it always did, high in the northern sky in its stagnant position, the dark eye glaring down on all of the Islands with a gaze that held little remorse for the children of the unpicked-lock. It was a most unwelcome union, but one which lit a fire within all thieves' hearts.

Demen was dressed as a travelling charms procurer. Bone fetishes and animal hides hung from his person like the tattered remains of some long-forgotten sailor's catch-net. By wearing such a disguise, he could avoid the unwelcome attention of the city watch, as it was considered an ill omen to accost such merchants on the eve of Nets. Only those sanctioned by the scriptures of the Watcher's benevolent gaze were exempt from such curses. And with the Hag's madness running through the Horogomy like wild fire, he doubted anyone would so much as glance at him let alone touch him. Unless of course they happened to be a Reaver witch-hunter and saw through his thin disguise to the Changeling beneath. The thought made him shiver and set his myriad collection of charms and borbals jangling.

The festival was the one time of the year when thieves were given free rein of the streets and, should they survive the night's festivities, they were free to leave with all their ill-gotten goods, unhindered by bounty or warrant. The catch was, there was always one in these types of affairs, that the Thief Catchers were also given free rein from the law and all its usual convenient bindings. They hunted any and all that they caught out on the night of Nets, and those that were caught would join the cities hanging tapestry of woe to remind all the price of their sins.

The poor fools currently being pushed and pulled by the sea breeze, from the high rafters above, were among the city's already condemned criminals. Their deaths were merely for decoration on this auspicious occasion. Demen slipped his way through the crowd, picking a few pockets as he went, as was his wont. There was an eruption of applause and Demen turned to find a group of acolytes of the Watcher's Catch temple making their way through the crowd carrying large fishing nets which they used to chase a crippled criminal down the street.

Demen hastily stepped aside as the congregation passed him by. As the thief lumbered past, he noticed that one of the poor fools knee caps had been busted in and the poor unfortunate had been stripped naked, his hide wet with blood and torn flesh from the torturers flails that had aided him in the confessing of his crimes and sins. As he understood the ritual, if the man reached the temple before he was caught by the acolytes measured pace, he would be freed on the spot and forgiven for all his crimes and sins. But, should he fail in his task, he would soon come to envy the twirling crows' feast dangling above.

Demen edged his way to the side of the street and settled into a small alcove in the shade as he let the grisly parade pass by. His heart was hammering in his chest, and an unknown and unwelcome sensation prickled his skin like flies over a four-day-old corpse. Would the cripple's fate be his own, should he be caught? He'd never experienced this type of fear for his profession before. He licked at his dry and chapped lips nervously. He was in an unknown place now. He had none of his pull with the authorities or with the local talent. He would need to tread carefully from here on out.

As he waited he half heartedly began to display his wares and mumble words about protection from ills and charms that would bless you in the Fishers ghostly light. So absorbed was he in watching the people pass him by that it took him a moment to notice the bedraggled figure standing to his left. He almost jumped out of his skin when he caught sight of the man or woman, he couldn't tell which, lingering close by.

"What?" he snapped at the androgynous stranger.

The stranger said nothing but pointed at a dangling bone charm that hung from Demen's little finger on his right hand. It was shaped like a dream-catcher and made of fish bones. Basesk swamp witches of the Sataran Isle claimed that the bone charms could hide a person from the eye of the Watcher when the wearer hid in the nightshade of the Fisher moon's opulent glint.

Still grouchy from the startle this beggar had given him, Demen gave a toothy grin and a sly smile as he said, "that one, eh? Fine, that'll be a half and three short bonds. But I doubt you've ever even seen that many hollows in your life, have ya? So I'll tell you what, I'll give you this piece of advice for free, in compensation for a goodly waste of my time." And he coughed for dramatic effect. "Piss off."

The stranger shot out a hand. Demen reflectively pulled away and put a hand at his back where he kept his short, curved gutter. He relaxed, though, when he saw that the beggar hadn't pulled steel on him, but instead held out a half and three short bonds in his or her grimy hand, the silver and bronze hollow discs shining dully in the wet shade of the looming building behind them.

Demen snatched the hollows from the beggar's hand, then thrust the bone charm into it with a snarl. Annoyed at being startled by the beggar for the second time, he turned his back without another word. When his preternatural nerves got the better of him, however he was forced to turn back, not trusting his back turned on such a creepy –

The beggar was gone. Demen could see no trace of where he or she might have fled to. Back into the crowd, most possibly. Well, good riddance, he thought letting himself slowly fall back to the tail-end of the streaming crowd while still half heartedly peddling his charms, not caring if anyone was interested or not. He decided to let the initial excitement pass him by, hawking his wares as was expected of him. He saw fellow charm merchants milling at the edges of the crowd. Like him, they too were keeping a healthy distance from the zealous Thief Catchers.

Pulling out a small brown bag and a pipe and silently cursing his shaking fingers, he filled the thing with a light-brown grass that smelled of charcoal, then pulled loose a smaller pouch from beneath his tunic and tattered travel cloak. This one contained his dust, known as huskerlyn or just husk. He couldn't walk through the capital smoking the stuff freely, but when mixed with a large amount of hash, the scent of the drug would be lost to the wind, so to speak. He'd only been in the damn city for little more than an hour, and already his nerves were on edge. He needed to claw back his usual economy of relaxed indifference, and his husk was just the thing to accomplish such a task.

Pipe between gritted and stained brown teeth and face hidden beneath his deep cowl, Demen followed at a slow pace and kept his gaze half on the large fishing nets ahead. At times he caught a view, through gaps in the buildings, of the higher levels of the city proper that was Al'Cier, looming above like some giant's hoard of silver coins teetering one way and then the other, the alchemical fires along its ramparts mimicking the stars in the slowly diminishing sunlight.

This wondrous quarter of the capital whose streets he was currently walking was known as Salt Breeze, the city beneath the city. Built upon the coast Salt Breeze had long ago been a fishing community and a place for pilgrims to come and marvel at the majestic wonder that was Donnardriss, home of the mysterious Cier, which covered the horizon to the east.

Al'Cier, also known as Highcrest or the seven jewels of the Horogomy, was built upon several rocky plateaus, flattened and reshaped over the years. It was here where the powerful and wealthy could feel a little less daunted by the colossal wonder that was Donnardriss to the east. At the very top resided the Ministry and the Royal Palace. One day, Demen thought, eyeing the glittering upper city, he would have to see if Highcrest was as impenetrable as some said. But not this day. He had a job to do on this day.

The parade ahead had picked up momentum now. The crippled thief had been snared by the acolyte Thief Catcher's, and they were carrying him to the Catch temple to roars of triumphant applause. The ghastly decorations had now been left behind and were replaced by thousands of nets draped from window to balcony. The harbour bells rang out in the distance to announce the approaching dusk and rising tide, but were slowly drowned out by the uproar of the crowd as they neared the temple courtyard.

The Catch Temple, once a brewery if his employer was to be believed, was untouched by any other buildings. A grand central square spread out before its mighty, looming walls. Enormous steel plates had been hammered into the dark-grey stone of the temple, and two large towers flanked the lower central building, which although smaller than the towers, was still an impressive four storeys high with a triangular roof of dark glass. Many alchemical fires burned along its ramparts in an assortment of gaseous colours, and on either tower there was draped a banner coloured in the orders regalia of white, purple and black. A single eye wrapped around a noose left little wondering as to the temples primary function.

At the steps leading up to the temples large darkwood doors, there stood a gathering of priests of the Watcher and a Judge of the Ministry draped in rolling folds of dark crimson, and wearing an ornate mask of gold that displayed an eternal look of disappointment. The procession stopped just before the grounds of the temple. Between the crowd and the temple was a wide, stone-paved square, where a gallows stood upon a raised stone altar.

Demen edged his way to the side of the crowd and settled himself against the wall of a double stairwell, one set of steps led down into a gutter alley, smells of dampness and sweet detritus assailed him and he felt a sticky film alight upon his tongue that not even his husk smoke could vanquish. Grumbling, he settled down on the cold steps of the other set of steps, which ran up the side of a tailors shop. From this advantage, he would be able to get a good view of the show.

The acolytes, carrying the crippled thief, met the Judge in the middle of the square before the gallows; a loud voice quietened the crowd with its authority and iron, clearly the voice of a noble born with its pinched and nasal arrogance. "Quiet!"

The punishment for interrupting a Judge must have been severe indeed for every voice that had, a moment ago, been crying out and calling for justice, was now suddenly silent.

"Until anointed in the sacred worship of our Lord of Justice and Judgment, you are all guilty in his almighty eye." The Judge ran a crooked finger along the crowd and Demen couldn't help but shiver when the clawed hand and masked gaze fell across him.

"On this night we defy all those that would slink and slither in the shadows of the Watchers darkened light to test our resolve. For this is the night of Nets! A sanctioned time when we tempt your faith and reward those who would be led astray by the Fisher's sickly illumination with the rope and noose of guilt's clear judgement. We will pull out his bloodied hooks from your flesh with holy screams and send you to the garden of the Hag's eternal darkness."

Nice speech, Demen thought. A little dry and tedious and a touch on the side of the zealous mad man for his tastes, though. But never-the less, the man got his message across. It might even have worked on some of the more cringing window creepers, but for the keen connoisseurs of lightened loads, it achieved exactly what it was meant to achieve. It was a challenge, a challenge to all those who thought they were above the law, or rather unseen by it.

And that was exactly what those bastard Catcher's wanted. For them, this night was as much about the challenge as it was the rewards. They wanted to pit their best against the streets best and, if possible, rid the world of a few more of its greatest thieves. It was said that the Patron Thief of the Fisher, the Master Thief, Denuden himself, had once come to the capital for the festival and stole all the nets before the night had even begun.

Demen didn't plan on doing anything quite as outrageous, but he did plan on spitting in those damned priests eyes while he was here. A raucous applause tore Demen from his thoughts. The crippled thief had been dragged up onto the altar. The Judge was speaking to the crowd once more.

"This," he said, gesturing to the semi-conscious thief, "is the price for all those who would stray from the path of righteousness."

The Judge raised one clawed hand; Demen found that even with his keen eyes he could not tell if the claw was a show piece or if it in fact was attached to the man's limb. With a snarl, the Judge rammed the claw into the thief's gut and pulled free his intestines.

An acolyte quickly moved forward, uncorking a vial of some sort, and wrenched the thief's neck back, forcing the contents down his throat.

The cripple's eyes snapped wide open and Demen found himself just as surprised as the thief must have been. He was still alive, and by the look on his face in great pain.

"The Watcher," the Judge continued, holding the man's entrails in his bloody claw, "does not allow those of the untrod path to simply stroll into the unholy garden of the Hag with such ease of passage. Life at this fresh hold is still his to command. Punishment must be met before a soul can slip into the Hags grasping thorns. Do not think that death will save you from His righteous hand."

The acolytes came forward and took the cripple under the arms, his moans of agony drowning out the sea winds. They lifted him up onto the gallows and tied the noose about his neck. Then, with his entrails still dangling from the unconcerned Judge's claw, they dropped the trap door. The crippled thief struggled for a time before the Hag's cold embrace came to rescue him from his misery. The cripple's death had been a grim affair. The man had lingered far longer than was natural and he had probably done nothing more than steal a loaf of bread. What then, would Demen's fate be, should they apprehend him on this night?

He scowled when he found that one of his hands had strayed towards a bone fetish hanging from his beard and was rubbing it between his fingers. Demen stood and made his way back into the crowd. The Judge also departed the stage, as the acolytes set about their ritual decapitation of the body. The cheers of the crowd grew louder with each swing of their axes, haunting Demen's every step.

He took room in an inn called the Narrow Staircase. The inn was conveniently located just across from the Catch temple. He took the attic room and gave the old lady a charm as he paid her for the night. She scowled at him and walked off in a huff, muttering about foul foreign beliefs. Once in his room, Demen rubbed a hand across the dust-smeared window and set his eyes on his intended target for the night.

Tonight every able-bodied priest of the Thief Catchers would be prowling the streets and rooftops for any and all who crossed their path, while the thieves of the city would be trying to avoid capture and secure themselves a nice, neat prize. Demen removed his disguise; he took out a razor and shaved his unkempt beard and hair until he was completely bald.

He then tore off his remaining rags and stood naked in the weak candle light of the narrow slanted room. Strange colours and shades rippled across his skin. As a Changeling he was endowed with a unique ability, that of adaption. Other Changeling's back in Mord called those of his talent's, Chameleons.

He stared back out the smeared window, at the lighted temple, the sun had now fully set and the alchemical wall lamps had been lit. Tonight, his prize lay in the vaulted cellars of the Catch temple. He didn't know what it was he was looking for exactly, but his employer had assured him that he would know it when he found it.

As the midnight bells sang out all across the city, thieves began to take to the roof tops, while the Thief Catchers left their temple, taking up their nets to begin the merry chase. The previous night's revelry had just been a warm up for the true festivities. Above, the Fisher's sickly light cast a ghostlike penumbra across the slick roof tiles. Demen, stood naked at an open window and let the cold air wash against his skin. When a cry like a slaughtered animal broke the silence of the night he smiled, for the Festival of Nets had begun.

# The Miracle, the Battle and the Dragon

## By Lynette Bishop

The tale ended. Each of us sitting round the fire fell silent and tears glistened in more than one pair of eyes. It was a moment before anyone spoke. The one to break the silence was Pinda, a big man, now folded to a comfortable size as he sat clasping his knees while the moon turned his dark beard to silver.

"Kel, will you give us the battle?"

Kel, that was me, and the story of the Battle of Cur Plain was the one they always asked me for. Tonight I didn't feel like telling it, didn't feel like  facing yet again the risk of what might happen.

"Aye, the dragon tale," demanded Heni, his eyes shining at the thought of danger, sitting safe as he was next to his mother. At nine years old he should not be speaking uninvited, but with everyone warm and at ease in the firelight, no-one minded. Except me. Perhaps I'd have more patience if I had children of my own. That was another thing I didn't want to risk but in this case it was within my control.

I reached for Nalia's hand. She squeezed mine and I minded less that, thanks to Heni, I'd not be able to persuade them to another tale and another teller. Once he had spoken it was too late, for in the red-gold glow of the flames I saw the faces around me light up as they imagined battles and dragons. They did this with no idea of the horror of battle or the nature of dragons. No-one here had ever seen either. Better that they had not.

"The battle tale it is then," I said, making no mention yet of dragons.

I waited a moment as the group settled with whisperings and shifting of position till they were ready, then I began.

"At a time gone but still remembered, a time when the stars were silent and the dragons slept, there was a miracle."

I paused there, as I always did, to let them dream. Life in the village was not easy and each one seated here had their own tale of hardship or loss. Each one hoped for their own miracle. In stories miracles can happen easily enough. In life they are hard to come by. What I described as one in my battle tale was perhaps no miracle at all. Tales always exaggerate the truth. They are only ever half the story.

"In the days when there were dragons," I went on, "there was peace throughout the whole land. In each kingdom was a wise, old dragon, counsellor to the king and protector of the people. The dragons were made by the Creator to be guardians of the whole world. Long before the first man was made, there were dragons."

Most of the people here, including young Heni, could probably have recited the tale from memory and yet, as I myself did, listening to the tales of others, they hung on every word. It was as if they were waiting to know what would happen next, a new thing they had never heard before. But the tale never changed. It was the same word for word as when I first told it more than ten years ago. It was not quite the same as the reality I experienced ten years before that when I, like Heni, was only nine years old and was there at the Battle of Cur Plain.

They all knew about Cur Plain. Many of then had been there, though of course it did not have the glamour of legend now as it had done twenty years ago. It had been, throughout living memory before that a vast, barren waste, bordered to the east and west by mountains, stretching north and south to an invisible distance. Nothing lived there except scorpions and other deadly creatures that no-one had been near enough to see close to and therefore to describe.

There was no source of water in the desert expanse. It was mostly hard rock, hot as the ovens in which bread was baked, and indeed anyone who ventured into the desert would soon end up burnt as a loaf which had not been taken out at the proper time.

It was believed that 'Cur', the name it was given, was a shortening of the word 'cursed', for that it certainly was. Its only virtue was that it formed a natural boundary, an uncrossable barrier between our kingdom and the next. If anyone was tempted to venture there a dragon would fly out and carry him back to the kingdom he came from. Our dragon, and probably the other, did this with words sharp as its claws so, that for a time no-one else dared make the attempt.

I described all this, and they sat quietly listening, even Heni, till I gave him the chance to speak.

"And so the flying of a dragon over Cur Plain came to be a sign that all men welcomed. It signified..." I let the words trail off and nodded to Heni.

"Peace!" he finished. "When you saw a dragon fly out over the plain, it meant there'd be peace."

"Well done, Heni, that's right. It was a sign of peace."

I smiled, Heni smiled and his mother smiled. Pinda, who had requested the tale, beamed. It was time to drop my listeners from a moment of light into the coming darkness of the story. I made my face grave and I went on.

"Some time past, a day came, a day that dawned like any other but was in the end like no day before or since."

Sitting in the balmy, evening air, I felt the storm that I was about to describe stirring. In reality I had seen nothing of it because my mother had gathered us all indoors and closed fast the shutters at the windows. Here I opened the shutters of the minds of those around me wide as the storm swept through my words. No-one wished to keep it out.

"First came the rolling clouds, billowing across the sky like a fleet of shadowy ships full of dark intent. They showered vicious torrents of rain as if the hands of giants holding enormous pails were emptying the heavens. Spears of light, so white they hurt the eye, were thrown by those same giant hands and the tormented earth groaned then roared in protest, splitting wide, belching out fire and hurling rocks through the blackened air."

I stopped and the silence dropped round us and we took a moment of respite, comfortingly held between one arm of the sleeping village and the other of the slumbering forest. Then I continued, describing the change that had come over Cur Plain.

Instead of hard rock and dusty earth there was an expanse of rich, brown soil which within weeks began to fill with plants, bushes, trees, grass - in fact, any green thing that could grow. No storm or earthquake could have made so rich a transformation and so people said it was a miracle, the miracle of Cur Plain. Looking back through the knowledge of the terrible events that happened afterwards, many questioned that the source of so much pain and death could be called a miracle.

"And so," I said to the circle of downcast faces, "while the land turned green, men's hearts turned black. Both kingdoms, ours and that on the far side of the plain, lay claim to the rich, fruitful land. The kings were swayed by evil men among their peoples and there were no dragons, full of wisdom, to counsel them."

That was a curious thing which had made men wonder at that time. When the storm and the earthquake finally ceased, the dragons were gone. Gone too, so it was reported, from other kingdoms across the world. People believed, or at least wanted to believe, that the dragons slept and one day they would come again. In the meantime, men began to fight for the land in the middle of Cur Plain which could not be easily allotted to one kingdom or the other. The fighting was turning to lawlessness as men crossed the plain, openly or stealthily. Attacks increased until the kings finally declared war.

The next part of the tale was hard to tell, for I remembered still my mother's anguish and my father's stoic silence which remained almost unbroken till the day he died. I told it anyway.

"One dark day the king sent a decree to every corner of our land and fear spread like a plague from village to village as the young men, some no more than boys, were summoned to the king's camp on a ridge high above Cur Plain."

My brothers, who knew nothing about killing men, when they were out of my mother's sight, brandished the new swords they had been given and laughed. To them it was a great adventure. I left that part out of my tale. What I said instead was true though, and nearer to what my listeners expected to hear.

"So, while mothers wept and fathers wrung their hands and bowed alone beneath the burden of their daily labour, the young men went bravely out to battle."

Now I was nearing the part of the story which was mine alone to tell which was true but strange. I had to take great care in the telling.

"There was a boy who had seen nine warm summers and lived through nine harsh winters. He walked out one spring morning at dewfall and arrived at the greatest adventure of his life."

Everyone knew, of course that the boy was me, and those older than I knew the winters and summers were not exactly as I described. The next part they would know was true, but what I described after that as I crossed field and forest could either be truth or the story teller's imagination.

"The boy was carrying, as was his mother's wish, a basket to his soldier brothers at the camp. It was the day before the Battle of Cur Plain, and in the basket were things to lift his brothers' hearts. His mother's cured meat, freshly baked bread, juicy fruit, sweet biscuits and a bottle of his father's garden wine. It was not an easy thing to carry across the meadows and through the forest, but the boy, stopping only when he had to change hands, did it gladly. He was eager to see his brothers, the camp full of soldiers and the fabled beauty of Cur Plain. He planned to be home by sundown.

"He was nearing the camp, almost at the forest's edge, when he heard the sound. It was hardly louder than the rustle of leaves or the faint tinkle of water trickling over mossy boulders into a stream but he heard it and knew it to be the sound of someone crying softly, a quiet, desperate sound. He dared not stop. His errand was too important. He could not arrive too late. The trees were thinning and he could glimpse the meadow and the rise of the hill beyond which lay the camp. But then the boy's heart turned cold for he could hear from over the hill other sounds, still faint but unmistakeable, the clang of sword on sword, shouting and screaming. Sounds he had never heard before but knew to be the noise of battle.

" 'No,' he cried. 'Not yet! Not till tomorrow,' and he began to run."

It was impossible for the group around the fire to be still at this part of the story. Pinda was on one knee, ready to rise. Heni was already on his feet with his mother scolding him and trying to pull him down.  They wanted, all of them, to go with the boy, to help in the battle, but they were twenty years too late. The battle was over. Only the sights the boy was about to see lived on. I kept them locked away behind a shut door in my memory most of the time. But you could not tell the tale without living it. I felt Nalia reclaim my hand and squeeze it once again.

"The boy moved desperately, as fast as his legs would carry him, out of the forest and  upwards past the boulders on the hill

"The hand!" Heni, to give him his fair due, had been good until now and even this outburst was of use, breaking the tension. Subdued laughter rippled through the group. Did he think I'd miss it! As if I could forget the hand.

"Then a hand came out of nowhere and seized his wrist. The basket went flying, everything inside it falling out and rolling away. The wine cracked open on a  rock and the red of it spilled over and onto the ground like blood. The hand was small but strong and the boy, caught off balance, went tumbling over. Flat on his back, he looked up into the pale face of a young girl. Her eyes were rimmed red from crying, but the boy gasped for they were of a colour he had never seen, like molten gold. Dark eyebrows furrowed over them. 'Don't go there!' she said, and he watched helplessly the tears well up and spill over. 'It's a terrible sight.'

"The boy's heart grew colder still at her words until it almost stopped.

" 'I have to go. My brothers are there,' he said.

"Without a word she took his hand and together they walked slowly up the hill. They stopped so he could only partly see and at a distance."

I decided for Heni's sake to keep the description as only the faint impression of what I saw. There was far too much horror for a nine year old boy. I did not tell them that I had to turn away to be sick and that after that, to my shame, I trembled like a girl.

"The boy turned from the terrible sight of men battling fiercely with each other. He did not know what he should do. Only when he felt the girl's hand on his arm did he look up. Her strange eyes were full of fear. She wrapped her thin arms round herself. She looked pitiful in her dress, also strange, which looked like green, plated armour, edged in red. 'I'm afraid,' she said.

"The boy nodded. 'Perhaps we should go.'

"He thought maybe he had no control over his heavy limbs. He tried to move but could not.

" 'I have to fly,' she said and her lip trembled.

" 'To fly?'

" 'It is the only way.'

"She was looking at him. The boy did not know what she wanted, what he could give her.

" 'Will you stand there?' She motioned beyond the tree to where the hill dropped into Cur plain. 'And watch me?'

" 'What?' The gory sights he had just seen filled his mind."

I glanced at Heni before continuing. Pinda had moved forward to place a reassuring hand on the boy's shoulder.

"He thought about his brothers and his stomach turned.

" 'Listen,' the girl said. 'There's no time to pity yourself while men are dying. I must fly. Will you watch me? If I fall, you must run. Someone must live to tell the tale.'

"The boy did not understand what she was saying but something deep inside him responded. He nodded. 'I will watch you.'

"The girl moved to the place where the hillside met the ridge and both fell away into Cur Plain. The boy found his legs supported him after all so he followed. There was no shield now between them and the battle, the noise and smell as terrible as the sight, the plain below not beautiful at all but dotted black with fallen men. The boy, looking down on the horror, missed the moment when the girl with a cry launched herself into the air.

"He stepped forward, nowhere near enough to reach her. She was already falling. He wanted to turn away but he had promised that he would watch. She became a small green speck, then black, no longer looking like a girl at all."

I paused. I think the group around me were forgetting to breathe. We were all seeing in our minds the girl in the last seconds before we lost sight of her, never to know why she had done what she did.

"Then the boy, unable to believe what his eyes were seeing, saw the speck stop in mid-air and begin rising again. Soon the black became green again and his eyes widened, distrusting what he was seeing. A dragon. He was seeing a small, green dragon rather shakily finding the strength of its wings. It continued upwards till, rising and dipping slightly, it was on a level with him. It looked at him, its golden eyes tinged with fear. It trod the air for a second, for long enough for him to realise what was needed of him and to cry out 'You can do it!' Then it flew.

"Out across the ravaged land it flew, riding the breezes till it was mid-way over Cur Plain. He did not take his eyes off it, for that was what he had promised. He became aware, though, of some change. It took him seconds to realise that the noise had stopped, the yelling, the screaming, the clashing of swords. There was silence. They had stopped fighting, it must be that. They were all watching the small dragon circling over the centre of the plain.

"It was something like a miracle, the boy thought. But it wasn't over. The small dragon was visibly tiring now. It had to come to rest somewhere, and that must surely mean coming within the range of the archers. They had stopped fighting because there was something they wanted more than the arable, fertile land of Cur Plain. They wanted the time of peace back again when the dragons ruled at the side of the kings and there was hope of happiness for all. But it would only take one man, wounded or angry or foolish enough to shoot an arrow, and the small dragon would fall and the battle would continue to its bitter end.

"The dragon turned, swooping towards him.

" 'Come on! You can do it!' the boy yelled."

"Come on!" yelled Heni. Everyone laughed then immediately grew tense again.

"Nearer and nearer came the small dragon until the boy could see its face but not its golden eyes. It was panting with exhaustion, its wing-beat slowing.

" 'Come on!'

"Just then, inches from the edge of the ridge, the boy saw something moving fast from the corner of his eye - an arrow."

It was Heni's mother, for a change, who reacted to this part of the story. She wiped her wet eyes with her sleeve. And she was not alone. At the sight I was conjuring up of the arrow flying straight towards the small, brave dragon, so near safety, many of the women cried.

"The arrow, a leaf's length away from the dragon's heart, was split in two by a second arrow, flying lightning-fast from the hand of an archer with a quick mind and great skill. The arrows fell, spiralling downwards into the void between the dragon and the land and the small dragon, in shock, dipped downwards following the arrows' fall.

" 'Come on,' the boy cried, and with no thought of his own safety, rushed to the very edge of the ridge. 'It's safe now. You can do it!' And he stretched out his hand even though the dragon was falling ever further out of reach.

" 'Come on.' He lay down on the stone-strewn grass, stretching his arm out over the edge, and his heart reached out too, hoping for another miracle.

"Slowly, as if each wing beat might be its last, the dragon began to rise. It faltered, rose again, almost fell, and all the while the boy repeated those two words, 'come on'. The fear that it was all in vain, that at any moment he would see the small dragon fall, was becoming too much to bear when suddenly the dragon, with a spurt of energy, rose level to the edge of the ridge and was there within the reach of his hand. Without knowing how to do it safely, he took hold of a  sharp claw to pull the exhausted dragon out of danger. He felt the dagger edge of claw turn into the moistness of a clammy hand, and the girl with the golden eyes sank to the ground at his feet."

I ended the tale then and came to the final sentences they knew so well.

"And after the battle of Cur Plain there were no more battles in the land. Even to our time. But neither was a dragon ever seen again. We are still in the time when the dragons sleep."

There was the customary moment's silence, broken once more by Pinda.

"Do you think, Kel, it's for us to make this a place the dragons will want to come back to?"

I tried to keep the surprise out of my face. It was the wisest thing I had ever heard him say. I felt Nalia squeeze my hand twice. I smiled.

"That's a good thought, Pinda. Perhaps it is."

And a strange thing happened. No-one asked for another tale. The whole group, even Heni, sat in silence.

After a while the fire died down and someone rose and stamped the embers out. 'Good-nights' were called out, but other than that no-one spoke as we turned each to our own home with only the starlight to show the way.

I put my arm around Nalia's shoulders. It had been wrong to fear that tonight would be different from every other time and somebody would guess. Perhaps soon it wouldn't matter if they did.

She smiled up at me, a twinkle in her golden eyes. "How surprised they would be if they heard the whole story of the Battle of Cur Plain."

I kissed her upturned face. "They wouldn't believe it if they did," I said.

## The Night Mist

## By David Trebus

Do not enter the mist, Edwin, they used to say. Avoid that small village when darkness falls, or you may never return; for fell things happen there during the night-time. Foul things only banished by the rising of the sun and the break of day.

They may as well have painted a huge sign saying "explore me" over that village by telling such tales to a young man such as I. Harriett, a fair maiden living down the street from me, had always said she liked brave men. Harriet had a reputation as unusual, some even called her a witch, not that I believed them. She had told me, were I to enter that lost village and bring her back a token at night, she would allow me to take her out for a drink and dance — and maybe more, if she liked me.

And so those moments led me there, standing at the threshold of Rogen, the lost village, just as the sun was beginning to set. Rogen had once been a regular trading partner to our own village, Rodden. After a fire started in the trading square, it had been reduced to a bunch of ruins and burnt outbuildings. That was when the rumours began.

Rumours of apparitions, of a creeping fog-like miasma that descended at night to consume those who entered the town. Some said the stories were to prevent looting, others to keep bandits from settling there. Others still said the rumours were to dissuade the younger members of town from going there to commit acts of carnality, unseen by their parents.

A wind blew up, causing a chill to run down my spine. I pulled my cloak around my hunched shoulders to keep the worst of the cold out, but being of slender build I always felt it, no matter what I did. My other hand gripped the length of wood I had taken with me for protection. The solid feel of it comforted me, giving me confidence in my ability to face any attackers.

The sun set behind me, and a fading golden glow briefly warmed my back before disappearing and leaving the cold chill of dusk. I waited at the threshold of the village, tense and nervous. I expected something to happen any moment, now the sun had set. I couldn't help but put some stock in the rumours I had heard. After all, it didn't hurt to keep an open mind.

Long moments passed, and nothing happened. I stood still as a statue, my ears straining and my eyes peering into the gathering gloom, but nothing alerted me to any danger. I begun to relax as the stories of the Lost Village, Rogen, faded from my mind and my confidence returned. There was nothing to fear here, just a ruin of a village lost to time.

I strode forward confidently, passing quickly over the village threshold, past a creaking sign denoting the entrance. That was when my confidence evaporated and fear again reclaimed my mind. The stories had not been simple rumours. Oh no, they were all very real, as I was discovering a little too late.

A thick fog formed along the ground, streaming from the dark doors and windows of houses and the shadows cast in the moonlight. The fog rolled towards me and around my feet, so thick I could not even see the ground I stood upon. I tried to rationalise what I was seeing. It was just fog, nothing untoward, but my instincts screamed danger.

Shapes began resolving in the distance, indistinct at first but becoming more and more solid. They formed straight out of the fog, figures made of billowing mist and vapour. They swayed where they stood, neither advancing nor retreating, mocking parodies of the human form.

I tried to back off, to step away from them but my back fetched up against something solid. I turned my head in panic to see a solid, white wall barring my exit. I felt along it, panic building, but it extended as far as I could see in both directions. The thought of being trapped only panicked me further, and I began to pound at the wall in frustration.

Hollow moaning rose upon the wind. A chorus of the damned, rising and falling in a song of despair and suffering. The wind blew, but the fog did not move, flowing with some malign intent of its own. I turned again slowly and regarded the scene playing out before me in the darkness, deciding to face the town in some last attempt at bravery.

The figures glowed in the night, casting faint green glows around them as they began to move. They ignored me as I stood there dumbfounded, frozen in terror, and went about their spectral business. They seemed to parody the movements of normal people, some tending non-existent animals, others setting produce on burnt-out stalls.

This play on daily village life seemed to go on for an age before it was interrupted. A commotion erupted, and the figures gathered together, their moans rising into wails. A ghostly woman, glowing blue, was led in front of a angry mob of green apparitions away into the village square. Curiousity overwhelmed good judgement, and my feet moved on their own to follow.

The blue glowing woman was surrounded in the centre by the mob, encircled. They threw small bits of mist at her, which dissolved into the air, yet the woman still recoiled as if struck. They paid me no heed as I crept up behind them and watched through their insubstantial forms as they assaulted the woman.

She was fair, even in her otherworldly state, her blue eyes like the noon sky, staring, staring straight at me!

Panic gripped me again as I stepped back and fell straight through another of the ghostly villagers. This one, however, was tinged red, his eyes following and glowing balefully at me as I fell through and behind him. He let out a loud scream that chilled my soul and froze me in fright, before a glowing red light formed in his hand, like a brand for cattle.

The red figure loomed over me, a stench of burnt meat creeping over to assault my nose and make me gag. He raised the brand over his head and seemed to grin, even as the crowd erupted in cheers. I shut my eyes, waiting for the moment that I became part of this ghostly mob, but it never came.

Another cry erupted, and I felt myself being borne aloft, as if flying or falling. I dared to open my eyes and saw the cool blue of the spectral woman staring down at me. She bore a look of love on her face, a look of concern and adoration, as she carried me, and my fear melted away in her embrace.

She passed straight through the barrier at the edge of the village, with no more effort than a man wading through water, and set me down on the other side. My legs collapsed under me, and I sat hunched and shivering on the ground, and looked up at her imploringly. Her figure flowed from the fog bank, connected by a thin stream; she was slowly being pulled back in.

"It is fine now my love, they cannot hurt you now. I would not tell them where you were. But to come for me was foolish. You should have stayed away; it was only me they wanted."

I had no reply for her. I just stared up at her, dumbfounded, even as I heard the cries behind the fog barrier grow louder and noticed a red and green glow form within it.

She simply smiled at me. "Do not fear. I will always protect you, even now, as they send me away because of my magic, but their sin will consume them, so stay out. Do not enter this village, unless you wish to join them in their burning prison"

The woman was pulled back in, a bright blue light joining the green and angry red. The lights danced behind the fog-bank, mingling as if in battle, until finally, just before dawn, they turned to flame. I felt heat against my face as I watched the village burn again, just as it had in the past. The fire consumed the fog just as the sun rose over the horizon, leaving only burnt-out buildings and the cold remains I had seen before.

I sat for long moments as the sun rose and the birds began to sing before I finally felt confident enough to move. My hand brushed against something as I made to stand up. A small, silver wedding band lay next to my hand. Immediately, I knew it had belonged to that woman.

I picked it up and ran, ran fast away from the scene of my terror. Ran straight into my village, past the dawn merchants setting up shops, past the shepherds goading their herds out to pasture. Straight into the arms of my lover, Harriett. She stared at me with cool, blue eyes.

Without thinking, I gave her the ring. It all seemed so strange but, at the same time, natural, and she smiled warmly when she saw it. We embraced and kissed in that same surreal moment, and I felt as if a presence looked over our newly kindled love. It was not long after that we were joined and you were born my, son.

So beware the lost village Rogen, for fell things dwell there, foul apparitions in the mist, awaiting those foolish enough to enter. I knew my son would likely listen for now, but when he got older I wondered if he would take the same path I chose, the path into the

mist.

# Tsukiko

## By Sandra Norval

Hisashi stood, knee deep in mud. He thought he was near the house but couldn't be sure. A scan of the area didn't help, it was all so different.

Just a few nights ago Tsukiko had smiled down upon him as they lay together, blissful. Her face glowed, a pale white light in the darkness, and he basked in her beauty. As she gazed at him he reached to her and stroked her skin. He had pursued her with a persistence that could not be beaten, captivated by her spell. He wanted her so much that to spend even a moment away from her left his flesh burning with desire.

Aware of his attention, Tsukiko carefully lowered her eyes whenever he was near, choosing to hide in shadows, away from his advances. The days were easy. She would remain out of sight, waiting for darkness, but at night she shone like a beacon, drawing him near without so much as a signal from her. Always respectful, he didn't touch, not quite. Always near, his spirit could reach hers even if his flesh could not, and she knew the fight could not last forever.

Eventually it came, the moment that their eyes met. He caught her as she moved from one room to another, and in her surprise she forgot to lower her gaze. She saw fire in his eyes which turned from the red of lust to a pale blue, a calm shade of love. It was the reflection of the fire in her own eyes, and she could fight no more.

He took her hand and led her to the garden. As they walked between the ponds, beneath the trees, she lit the way and he bathed in her glow.

"I shall tell you of my ancestors," he said as they stood under the cherry tree.

Tsukiko smiled. How she longed to hear of his ancestors, as hers had long been forgotten. She wasn't even sure if there had been any. With a nod, she knelt beside him in the soft dewy grass and waited for his tale to begin.

Hisashi knelt before her and took her hands in his, kissed them, never once releasing her gaze.

"My family is honourable. We are the protectors of the Earth, and we are here to hold back the waters from the homes of our people. I have lived these last three centuries alone, entrusted with the safety of the homes of all the families here. But I do not wish to be alone any longer. Tsukiko, I wish for you to be my wife and live with me here forever."


Her smile faded, and the garden seemed more than a little darker. Her eyes filled with tears and her hands began to tremble. Hisashi gripped them tighter, afraid to let go. She peered into his eyes, as the tears brimmed over. The fire in his eyes turned yellow, then orange, then red, and she snatched her hands away to cover her face. As she curled on the grass she began to sob. She was just half the size of him, and to run would be futile.

Hisashi recoiled, disgusted with himself. He watched her, broken in the grass, then stood and turned away.

"You are free to go if you wish," he whispered, "but I wish with all my heart that you would choose to stay."

"I cannot," she said. "To stay would mean the end for us all."

He didn't understand. Burdened with sadness, he watched her run until she disappeared behind the mountain.

The day passed by slowly and Hisashi stood watching the mountain, hoping she would return.

Dusk came and he didn't see her appear. A tap on his shoulder jolted him from his vigil and he drew his sword, spun around and froze when he realised that he was about to strike down the woman he had been waiting for. She drew a breath, held it, brought her hands up and clasped them palm to palm around the sword.

"Hisashi, I have returned, but if you wish me dead, so be it." She released the sword and straightened herself up, ready to receive the blow should he choose it. She stared into his eyes and watched the flame return to blue. She exhaled as the weapon clattered to the floor.

"Tsukiko." He cupped her face in his hands as he whispered her name. "I would never harm you."

She gave herself to him that night, unable to hold back any longer.


\*\*\*


"Ah, Tsukiko, remember that day when we stood beneath the cherry tree and it sprinkled petals in your hair?"

"Of course I remember!" she giggled and brushed his hair from his face. "It was only yesterday, how could I forget?" He revelled in the delicate movement of her body on his as she laughed. Her skin on his. He wrapped his arms around her and pulled her closer for another kiss. Her silken hair brushed his face, and a thrill ran through him.

It had been a night of perfection, but she drifted away when daylight came and, though he clutched at her, begged her to stay, she turned and stared deep into his eyes.

"I cannot," she said. "To stay would mean the end for us all."

Again he didn't understand, and with a heavy heart he released her.

The next night he waited again, watching for her, this time with his back to the mountain. He saw her appear on the horizon, her glow lighting her way back to him. She ran to him, and they made love over and over until the night was done and daylight began to return.

Exhausted, Tsukiko lay asleep in Hisashi's arms. He looked at her, ran his hands over her body and decided to let her sleep for a little longer. As the sun rose and the first rays touched her skin, she screamed and leapt up, cowering in the remaining shadows. Hisashi jumped up and reached for her.

"Tsukiko, what is it?" She looked at him, and he saw her eyes were wide with fear. She shook her head and held her hands in front of her face as if he had raised his hand to her.

"Keep away! Do you know what you have done?" As he stepped closer, she cowered and crumpled to the floor, wailing.

"I did nothing wrong, you were asleep, I didn't want to wake you."

"And in doing so you have destroyed us all." Hisashi clutched at his breaking heart, still confused at what he had done.

"Run from here!" she screamed. "The age of man is over. You must run, for the sea is coming for you."

He took one more step towards her and she raised herself up, defiant. She pointed at him and, in a calm steady voice, she chanted.

"You are the Earth, I am the Moon, between us lies the sea. You are the Earth, I am the Moon, between us lies the sea." Hisashi started to move towards the door, blinking in the sunlight. He turned back to Tsukiko, but she was beginning to burn. The chant went on and, as she glowed brighter, he turned and ran to the village to save those he was born to protect.

A breeze brushed past his ear and her voice whispered on it.

"I was the barrier for the sea, it was for me to pull it back and forth to protect you. By meeting the sun, I failed. Run, Hisashi, run."

Just behind the wind came the water, rushing in, forcing its way between the mountains, washing away the village and anything else in its path. Hisashi and the people he had saved sat on the mountain, watching the swirling waters carrying away the lives they had toiled to build.

They stayed on the mountain until the waters receded. Hisashi returned to the village and found just mud. He looked to the sky and thought of Tsukiko.

A breeze brushed by his ear, and he heard her sigh, "Hisashi."

# On a Nameless

# Shore

# By Nyki Blatchley


on a forgotten frontier
between the sea and the tideline
cliffs behind me seem to support the clouds
surrounding me with faces like dark glass

and the sea is never still
and its call is never silent
and the clutching waves that gurgle seductively
have toiled across a thousand miles to find me

there is no sky out here
only a boiling roof of dark
and I have no lodestone that can tell me
whether the call is coming from east or west

a boat tosses its prow
coquetting me to sail
out to where the storms grotesque explosion
tumbles a lover to the limitless ocean

## The Heat-Death Of The Ocean
## By Nyki Blatchley

drifting somewhere
                    downwind of the World-Tree
an ice-floe
            edges
                    dreamward
unrepeatable
                    crystaline clarity
calling to the battered hulk
                        [holed but whole]
that sniffs out a path
                    across twisted fields
                                of Arctic flame
flaring like a sunburst rockets
                            spatter-shower
            to seek and find
[cruising as fire on a dark wind]
the hidden breach
                    in the blue of the bailey-wall
the sudden burning
                    of a south-giant
                                consuming
passion of snowfall
                        burning the wind
until ice-dragons
                        saturate the sky
and freeze fire
                        as it falls
too little
        too long to live
                    in the arid choke
                            of dry blaze
living light

                    in ice
                                loosed to flow
                                            the hound howls
                                            the wolf runs
                                            battle joined
                                                        between clarity


and haze
burning the world
                                into tepid muddy water
to wash away
                                memories of perfection
leave unending shifts
                        that lift
                                    the broken barquentine
out onto untrammelled ocean
                                            to founder in storm-wrack
                                            or find safe sublimity

# RETURN SWITCH

## BY NYKI BLATCHLEY

"There's been another one." Sergeant Kuruk raised his head from the comm-ball, a blend of anger and disgust etched on his broad face. "Just three blocks from here, Inspector."

Rising from behind his desk, Inspector Davilon Hirghe cursed with the fury and helplessness that always overcame him at such moments. "That's the fourth this week." He walked around to look over the sergeant's shoulder at the ball. "Details?"

Kuruk hesitated for an instant before swallowing. "Just a kid." His eyes were fixed on his inspector. "Fifteen-year-old girl, snatched like the rest."

At once, Davilon was drowning in horror and despair, back at the moment he'd been told about Naryth. No, he needed to focus on this case. He met Kuruk's eyes, but the sergeant avoided eye contact. Kuruk must have seen pretty much everything in his thirty years on the force, but he looked pale.

None of Davilon's officers seemed to know what to say to him in these situations, and he hoped fervently they wouldn't think of anything. Taking refuge in procedure, he snapped, "Witnesses?

Any description?"

"One of those things with the scales and teeth. Just appeared in the street, the witnesses say, and grabbed the girl. Seemed random. Vanished before anyone could move. Most of the witnesses are being treated for shock."

Davilon nodded, sucking air through his teeth. *With the scales and teeth* – yes, no need to elaborate on that. No-one knew what they were actually called – the whole situation was too new for genuine information – but the media had dubbed them the scalies, and they were the most dangerous of all the demons now preying on the streets of Sargil. Some of the others could be stopped if you got very lucky, but scalies were in and out of reality too quickly, even if you were there with a drawn weapon.

"Parents been informed?" he asked, half hoping they had been, though he never ducked this duty. He'd found out about Naryth by reading her name in an anonymous report. No-one else was going to get the news so casually, not on his watch. In any case, looking the victim's loved ones in the face gave him the determination to do whatever he could to stop these atrocities. Or more.

"Haven't been tracked down yet, sir."

He nodded. "Let me know when they have, Kuruk, and sort

out the details. I'll give a briefing in half an hour."

Nodding, the sergeant input the activating spell on the printer attached to the large crystal ball. Magical energy crackled around it, and print was appearing on the blank sheets as Davilon left the office.

*****

They should have asked for his I.D. at the door of the Magitech Institute, and Davilon considered reprimanding the security guard for waving him through. Then again, this man knew him well enough. He'd visited the Institute regularly since the Event, six months ago, hoping against hope to get early word of some breakthrough offering hope in this losing battle.

The visit to the victim's family had been harder than usual. Vavri Shorlu, her name was, her parents' only child. There'd been pictures of her everywhere in the living-room, from a grinning imp, all messy red hair and freckles, to a teenager who looked as if not smiling would be an effort. Not especially like Naryth, but the same kind of energy and joy, and only a year older.

It had been the father, a large, dependable-looking man, who'd cried silently, while the mother, who looked like an older version of Vavri, had raged at Davilon for not doing more to protect her child. Unfair though it was, he'd let her abuse him. Perhaps it helped.

His wife had been the same when their daughter was taken, only a few weeks after the Event. It hadn't even happened in his area of the city, but it was his job to stop it, she told him. It was all his fault. After a week of abusing him, she'd gone to her parents and refused to return his calls.

There was nothing to be learnt at Vavri's home – the demon attacks appeared entirely random – and he wanted to feel he'd done something before returning to the police station. That was why, as so often, he'd come to see Professor Burrighe to find out if there'd been any progress.

"Shut the door," Burrighe's voice yelled. Davilon ducked instinctively, just in time to avoid the fireball that crashed into the wall behind him, leaving the stench of charred plaster.

"That's a fine welcome," he commented. "Something I said?"

"You changed the room's psychic balance," the professor snapped. "What do you expect? I'll have to set that up all over again."

Burrighe looked every inch the eccentric scientist, with wild grey hair and thick glasses, but Davilon knew everything he did, both in and out of the laboratory, was meticulously planned and calculated.

"What, shooting a fireball? Every rookie officer under my command can do that."

The other man snorted without apparent malice, clearly knowing he was being teased. "Without needing a thrower?"

"No tech, you mean?"

Davilon was genuinely impressed. Developing magic that worked without tech was an ideal of scientists. Every so often, the media would get hold of a half-true claim that someone had developed it; it would be a sensation for a few days, till someone else debunked the idea. Still, it was worth hoping. Perhaps, if it could be achieved, they wouldn't be quite as helpless against the demons.

"Not quite." The professor took off his glasses and cleaned them with careful precision. "I still need one device, but I'm working on bypassing it." He put the glasses back on and glared at Davilon. "I'm assuming you haven't come about that part of my work, Inspector."

Davilon sighed. "I don't know why I've come, really. It all seems so pointless, sometimes."

Burrighe nodded. "Another one? They're getting more frequent, aren't they?"

"And more widespread. At first, only the city centre was affected. Now they're common in the suburbs, too, and there's been a case in Corcash. Everyone's panicking. At this rate, it'll be all over the country in a few years. Then... who knows?"

"We're all working on solutions." The professor began cleaning his glasses again, then stopped and looked at them, as if puzzled. "It would help if we knew what the Event was."

That was one of the key problems. The magical explosion that had torn holes – tiny at first, but growing – in the fabric of reality had come and gone so quickly that no-one could work out what had caused it. Theories had ranged from a badly malfunctioning domestic device to a terrorist attack, but the most likely one was a home-researcher's experiment gone badly wrong. The apartment block at the epicentre had vanished, so there seemed little chance of finding any clue to what the experiment might have been.

"That won't save the victims, though. This one's only fifteen, and I'm trying not to imagine what she's suffering now. She might still be alive, but there's no way of rescuing her."

As there'd been no way of rescuing Naryth. Most people

assumed the victims died quickly. The thought offered what scant comfort there might be, but Davilon couldn't believe it. Since all accounts agreed that the demons never harmed their prey before vanishing, it seemed likely they kept them alive. For a while, at least. That made his impotence even harder to bear.

Burrighe jammed his glasses back on and fixed Davilon with his eyes. "Because the place is full of demons? Or what?"

Davilon flung up his arms in an extravagant gesture. "They die if you hit them with a thrower. That's not what I mean. We don't even know how to get to wherever she's gone."

The professor was silent for a moment, his eyes calculating as if solving a mathematical problem. "You'd do it, if you could? Follow them where they take the victims?"

"Faster than a lightning-caster." Was this just academic questioning? "Why?"

"I think," said Burrighe slowly, "I have something that might interest you."

*****

Davilon stared back at the two dozen faces gazing at him, struggling to gauge whether their silence was acceptance or denial. He'd made clear he was asking for volunteers only. These were officers he'd trust with his life – had done on a number of occasions – but how would they react to this proposal?

"This device?" Jashek was always the first to raise objections, but that was fine. She was right to be cautious, and it didn't stop her from acting decisively when she needed to. "Just how reliable is it?"

"I haven't a clue. It hasn't been tested in the field." He met Jashek's eyes firmly. "Look, I'm not going to lie to you. This isn't a safe option. Professor Burrighe is *pretty* sure it'll open up the last slip in a given location. Not a hundred percent, but pretty sure. What we don't know is the conditions we'll find there. We'll have to improvise and hope we don't hit a demon hot-spot."

"What about getting back?" Jashek was fiddling with her sleeve, as she always did when she was going through what could go wrong. "It's not going to do the kid much good if we're all stuck there, is it?"

There were a few mutters, but Davilon couldn't tell if they were agreement or censure.

"Good point," he cut in quickly. "Burrighe says all the test animals came back after exactly fifty-eight and a half minutes."

"Alive?" someone called out.

He shrugged. "The smaller ones. When he sent larger creatures... well, they must have been more visible to the demons."

"So we'll have to survive there for nearly an hour?" Jashek asked. "Could be tough, depending on how many hostiles we're facing."

Davilon shook his head. "The automatic return will be a back-up," he said, "but Burrighe's got a manual return switch working. We can bring ourselves back when we're ready."

The professor had described in proud detail how he'd strapped the device to a mouse, with a piece of cheese positioned so that the mouse would activate the switch when it managed to get its treat. The mouse had been back in two minutes.

"How many are going?" asked someone at the back. "How many of those things did you get?"

"This is the prototype. The only one." A murmur rippled through the crowd. "Burrighe reckons it'll take us all, as long as we're touching. There may be a limit, but enough of us should get through."

"Why can't we have one each?" Jashek demanded.

"Because it'll take at least three days to make any more." This was dragging on too long, and they were having time to get scared. "Look," he said, "like I said, this is dangerous; but there's a sweet young girl being tortured by demons, and we've the chance to bring her back. I'm going. Anyone coming with me?"

The silence lasted about two seconds before Jashek said, "Me." It took a bit longer, but the whole unit volunteered at last.

*****

"I think it was here," said Sergeant Kuruk, casting about on the pavement. "The witnesses mostly agreed it was outside the bottled imp shop."

"Mostly?" someone queried sceptically, and a ripple of laughter eased the tension for a few seconds. They sometimes took light-hearted bets on how many of the witness statements from a case would agree, and Davilon was glad to see their humour hadn't been squashed by what they were doing.

A small crowd looked on curiously from behind the barrier set up for the investigation, though people tended to stay off the streets as much as possible. Apart, that was, from those whose solution to panic was to smash windows and loot shops. The specialist Trackers, whose machines recorded the psychic imprints of a crime scene, were also behind the barrier. Even they seemed confused at a squad of fully armed officers, fireball throwers primed and ready for use, gathering on the spot.

61

"Right," said Davilon, "Burrighe said it would work within about three yards." He positioned himself halfway along the shop-front. "This should be close enough."

He glanced at the commander of the Tracker unit, who nodded.

"Now, we need to be touching. We don't know what we're going to find, so safety off your throwers." He took a deep breath, checking they were all linked. "All right, let's go and get Vavri."

He flicked the switch on the small box strapped to his arm and set the activating spell in motion. Magical energy crackled around his hands, but he hung onto the box, praying enough of the squad would be transferred to be of use.

Davilon heard Kuruk, next to him, swallow hard as the tingle of the wave-front spread outwards, growing in intensity until it reached a spot just to his left. Like water finding a plug-hole, the magic poured into the place, tugging everything in its wake. Davilon's body was pulled and twisted, as if he'd been hit by a disruptor, and he felt his etiolated form diving into the hole.

Then all was back to normal, except for a wave of heat on his skin and a sense of horror assailing him from all around. Everything he could see glowed a dark red, and something howled behind him.

He was alone.

He'd deal with that later. Whirling, Davilon found a demon rushing at him, jaws wide to reveal teeth as long as his hand. Too close to use his thrower. Yanking out his side-arm with his left hand, he sent a beam of searing magic into the thing's chest, and it collapsed.

He glanced around, taking stock of his surroundings. This was a land of barren rock and ash, stretching away in an uneven plain, but the air's intense, deep-red glow coloured everything to make the landscape seem to be burning. Beyond the red, darkness loomed, as if the whole place were enclosed in a cave.

Here and there, Davilon could make out demons, all scalies like the one he'd just destroyed, lounging on the rocks. Several were watching him closely, but made no attempt to attack. Were they wary of his weapons, or just waiting for him to come closer?

So Burrighe had been even more wrong than he'd anticipated. It seemed the device could only transport one person. Fine, when everyone had their own, but that wasn't going to help him now. He could return any time he liked – assuming the return switch worked, of course – but he'd be giving up the only chance of rescuing Vavri. By the time more of the things could be made, it was doubtful there'd be enough of her left to save.

On the other hand, he might be too late now. There was general agreement among the researchers that the demons probably didn't kill their victims straight away, but no-one really knew. He couldn't believe anyone survived for long in this place.

Was this where Naryth had been brought? Back then, it had been difficult to identify the different types of demon, but the sketchy accounts from traumatised witnesses suggested it had been a scaly. Perhaps one of these creatures lounging on the plain had killed his daughter.

That decided Davilon – he'd look around for Vavri, with the return switch as insurance. There was always the danger of being taken off guard, but he hadn't expected this to be a safe mission.

He scanned the desolate, crimson-tinged landscape for any sign of a human. Nothing obvious, except... What was that brute pawing at? Narrowing his eyes against the glow, Davilon strained to see what lay in a little hollow beneath one of the scalies. Was that a hint of human flesh?

He hesitated a moment longer, looking around to fix the position of each demon. There weren't any very near. Perhaps – he shuddered – they preferred to be alone while they tormented their victims. Or fed.

The last thought propelled him forward, but he moved

slowly for fear of rousing any of the other scalies, thrower cradled against his right shoulder and the sidearm in his left hand. He had around a hundred yards to go and, while none of the creatures was on his route, he passed closer to one than he liked. It looked as if it might be sleeping, but he couldn't be sure.

The demon stirred as he skirted around it, but didn't lift its head. Davilon tiptoed on, casting regular glances back to see if it had woken, until he was within ten yards of his target. The scaly looked up from what was occupying it.

Its charge was so quick that Davilon just had time to raise his sidearm and shoot before it was on him. The beam only caught it a glancing blow, but that was enough to knock it backwards off its feet. Before it could recover, he dropped the small weapon, swung the thrower into place and sent a fireball into its guts. Its body exploded in flames.

Running past the burning demon, he found himself looking down into a shallow dip where Vavri lay. His immediate relief that she still lived was quickly swallowed by horror at the state of the girl. Her clothes had been almost completely ripped off, and her body was covered with bruises and lacerations. The impudent face from the picture was swollen with tear-streaks through the dirt, and her blackened eyes stared out, flat with terror.

"Vavri," he said, struggling to keep his voice gentle as he

crouched beside her, "I'm Inspector Hirghe. I've come to take you home."

She stared blankly at him, but tried to move and gave a little scream. For an instant, Davilon wasn't sure why, till he realised her right hand was fixed to the ground by a stone spike right through it.

"Vavri, I'm going to pull this out." He kept his eyes on hers, but she didn't react. "I'm sorry, it'll hurt, but I need to get you free."

She still made no response, so he set his teeth and pulled at the spike. The girl screamed louder as it slid out of her hand.

That had done it. Glancing around, Davilon saw a dozen or more of the closest demons rising to their feet, turning toward them. Time to go, he thought, reaching for the return switch...

And the reality came crashing in on him: if the device only transported one person here, how much chance was there of it taking them both back?

He looked at Vavri. The girl was clutching her bleeding hand, but otherwise showed no flicker of emotion. For an instant, Davilon wondered how much point there was in taking her home. Could she really ever recover from what she'd suffered here?

No, it didn't matter. She might be in the hands of the

psychomages for the rest of her life, but while there was any hope, he had his duty. Given the choice of having Naryth back, even in such a state, he'd have had no hesitation.

Should he try to attach the device to both of them, in the hope that would fool it? No, too risky. If it did only take one, he had to make sure it was the girl. He'd have to hope that, if he was holding onto her, he'd be taken too. Otherwise, could he stay alive till the automatic return kicked in?

Kneeling beside Vavri, he tugged the device from his arm and wound the strap round hers. There was no time to make it secure, but it would do.

"Vavri," he told her urgently, "press that switch." He touched it with his fingertip, but she didn't even turn her head to look. "Vavri, you've got to..."

There was no time; the demons were almost on them. Grabbing the girl's hand – her injured one, making her scream – Davilon forced her finger down on the switch and hugged her to him. The wave of magic built at once, and he clung onto her. Vavri screamed again, perhaps feeling the suck of the magic, and vanished from his grasp.

Pushing himself to his feet, Davilon swung around in a circle, shooting off fireballs continuously at the demons that came at him.

If he could just escape from them, all he'd need was to play hide-and-seek for nearly an hour.

The thrower jammed. Examining it wildly, Davilon saw he'd exhausted the spellcaster. He had a spare, but it took nearly a minute to replace, and the side-arm was out of reach on the ground. He was going to die here, in the same wilderness as his daughter.

The demons crowded around, claws slashing. Hot, foetid breath swept over him as long, razor-sharp teeth met in his neck, and his last thought was that at least whatever was left of his body would return. He wouldn't be left lying in this terrible place.

That was good.

# The Giant

## By David Trebus

It loomed over me, a towering shadow of monstrous proportions. It exuded malice and threat, the darkness of its form only adding to my fear. My instincts kept screaming at me to run away, to turn aside and flee as far as I could, to somehow escape from this giant of shadow.

I tried my hardest to make out details of its composition, somehow gain knowledge to help dispel my ignorant fear and bring me some understanding of just what this thing was. The bright light cast from behind the form kept preventing me from doing so, obscuring its detail, beyond the fact it was vaguely humanoid in shape.

Yet somehow my imagination kept attempting to fill in the blanks. I pictured glowing, red eyes, filled with hatred and a desire to destroy. I envisaged a huge maw of serrated teeth, open wide in a silent scream. And, finally, I imagined an evil presence, waiting with malign patience for its prey to come closer. All of these imagined details seemed to take shape on the dark canvass that was the giant, and finally my nerves could take no more.

I turned to run, run as fast as my legs could take me. I pushed my body to its limit, breathing heavily as my muscles burned with effort. My brow streamed with sweat as I panted and kept running, too scared to even cast a glance backwards. Yet, as I ran, the shadow cast by the figure never diminished around me. The shadow stretched off into the distance before me in a hazy, grey landscape of dark clouds and featureless rocky ground.

My body finally gave up long before my will to escape did. I collapsed on the ground, my chest heaving to suck life preserving air into my burning lungs. I lay there waiting for the inevitable, for that dark form to descend upon me and devour me, ending my suffering. I wondered how long it would take it to catch me. With such giant legs, it would surely be soon. I squeezed my eyes shut tight, waiting.

But the moment never came. I waited in silence for what seemed like hours, but in reality could have only been minutes, or maybe even seconds. Nothing happened, other than my breathing easing as my body recovered from its exertions. I eventually opened my eyes, wondering what was going on. I stood up shakily and looked in front of me. The shadow cast by the giant had not changed; it stretched off into the distance still. I turned round, forcing my eyes against all my animal instinct to look upon the form again.

To my surprise, it had neither advanced nor diminished. The towering shadow remained exactly the same size as it had before, cast against brilliant light behind it. I kicked the dusty ground in fear-induced rage. It seemed there would be no escape, no quick end, even if I ran or if the shadow caught and put an end to my terror.

My anger built inside me, and I felt frustration like I never had before. "How the hell can I get away from you?!" I yelled impotently at the looming form. My protestation provoked no reaction, no response, other than my words echoing back to me like a parrot's call. "I can't handle this," I mumbled, almost in tears.

I tucked my legs up against my chest and huddled myself into a little ball for comfort, wrapping my arms around my knees to pull them in close. I remembered all the times in the past I had felt like doing just this but had not been able to. My emotions were a whirlwind of past regret and deep-seated frustration. I just couldn't understand what was happening.

Then a single thought struck me. It felt almost like a physical blow to the head. I could end up here all my life, stuck, closed up in a little, human-sized ball of fear and sorrow, hiding and running in the shadow of a malevolent giant. The thought filled me with even more dread and anguish as I pondered its consequence. Living a life in shadow was really like living no life at all.

Then a second mental blow came. A tiny voice whispered on a non-existent wind, "You've always been here, you just didn't realise it". This was almost too much, as I just couldn't avoid the truth of the statement. Somehow, I knew it was right, that I had always been living in the shadow of the giant. Again I wondered how I could escape, feeling at my most desperate.

Then the third thought came. I did have a choice in the matter. One I would have never even have considered before. The sheer madness of the idea felt liberating, but on some deep level I knew it was the right thing to do. It was just something I hadn't felt I had the strength to do in the past.

I stood up, shaking slightly, wiping a tear from my eye. I turned around to face the giant, feeling defiant as I prepared myself for what I had to do. Fear filled my limbs but, instead of using it to flee, I began running, running straight towards the giant with all its shadowy glory.

I ran, laughing like a lunatic, straight into the shadow of that giant form, terrified beyond all reason but still somehow, on a primal level, knowing I was making the right choice. As I ran towards it, instead of growing larger, the giant began to shrink. Its proportions grew smaller and smaller as I approached it, and the light behind it grew brighter.

I slowed my pace as I approached, jogging to a stop in front of a normal-sized person, a person I could see clearly now. I looked at my reflection, terror in it's face, but the same wide-eyed determination to be accepted and move forward. I didn't know what to do, so I let my instincts take over. I jumped forward and embraced myself, pushing us both into the shining light behind.

I embraced the giant, I embraced the fear, I embraced myself and cast myself into the light.

## Halfa House
### By Sandra Norval

We walked past it every day, the house with half a house hanging off it. You'd have thought it would cause structural problems, but it stood firm. Heck, there was even a family living there. Well, not in the halfa house. That's what we called it. We weren't very imaginative as kids.

It's been over three decades since I've been here but there it is, suspended above a patch of wasteland. My mind wanders a little; surely by now someone would've built a house here. No, a block of flats more like and no parking to go with them. I find myself tutting. That's London I'm thinking of. No-one wants flats here. No-one wants anything here. So it stays, the halfa house.

I remember the jagged edges of the floors; not a single brick has fallen, not a plank is out of place. It's as if someone has cast them in glass or something. Solid enough to freeze it in time but clear enough to see every splinter.

I know I should get back. People will be waiting. I don't want to go back. Here I can pretend that she's still with me, holding my hand.

"Dare you to climb up to the first floor," she whispers in my ear, but I know she isn't really here. Not this time. I shake my head. I never did take her up on the dare, but she didn't marry me for my courage. Good job, really.

"Go on," she goads me, "do it for me." I can feel her fingers in my hand and can't help but give them a squeeze. "You never did, did you?"

I suck in a breath and exhale, long and slow. It ends with a raspy cough. That never used to happen. I draw a hand slowly across my face, wiping away the years.

She tugs her hand from mine, and I catch a glimpse of her ducking through the gap in the fence. I hear her laughter brought to me on the dusk breeze. Peering into the yard, I am certain I see her. It's the light playing tricks, I'm tired, I'm grieving. But still I follow.

I feel the chicken wire scrape across my shoulder and I know I've drawn blood. It's not the first shirt I've ruined playing her silly games. The crisp white fabric turns crimson, and I watch the patch spread in the failing light. I sigh, commit myself and drag the rest of my sorry body through the gap.

My hands are smarting, the gravel sticks to the blood that's coming from them and I can't help but laugh at myself. What a bloody idiot. Scrabbling through this wasteland, pursuing the same woman that led me through here all those years ago. It was different then, I could keep up with her.

I brush the gravel away as best I can and look across the scraps of grass towards the house. She's there, staring at me, smiling. I smile back and start to walk towards her. With every step comes another memory of this place. That first fag we'd shared, the bottles of cider we used to pass around, our first kiss. The first time I touched her. The first...

I shake my head again and clear my throat. I want to clear her out, but she's still here, clinging on. I look back to where she was a moment ago, but she's moved. She's on the staircase. It stops halfway up; it's got everything, even two flying ducks on the wall. Beneath the stairs is the rusty carcass of an ironing board, an old wooden clothes horse and some other bits and bobs that were there when the house came down. She's laughing and calls to me.

"Come on! You never even made it this far, did you?" I curse under my breath. She knows I am scared of heights. Standing on the edge of those stairs is probably my worst nightmare. Except it isn't. Losing her is my worst nightmare. I am compelled. I have to reach her before she falls. I can't lose her again.

So I run. I run across the rubble between me and the house to save her. I step into the house and the breeze stops. I turn, and somehow the rest of the house is behind me.

I'm standing on a rug, one of those heavily patterned things with tassels on the ends. The stairs go all the way now, the ducks are flying all the way up the wall leading me to the top of the stairs, to her.

Stomp, stomp, stomp.

Her footsteps move across a bare wooden floor, out of sight upstairs. I step around the sofa and stand at the foot of the stairs, staring up. There's a light on. I stagger back and knock over a mustard-coloured standard lamp. I catch it mid fall, and the tassels swing back and forth. I want to stop them, it proves that I'm here and I know I shouldn't be. I stand the lamp back on its base and slowly release my hands, testing it, making sure it's balanced. I step back and turn to face the stairs.

"I'm waiting!" she calls in a sing-song voice.

I reach for the banister and grip it firmly. My mouth has gone dry, and I try to swallow, but it's like I have a golf ball in my mouth. I plant a foot on the bottom step, swallow again and draw a breath. It creaks as I shift my weight onto the front foot. The second step creaks too. I work my way up the stairs and try to remember how many steps she used to count before the top. No, not the top, the halfway, the point where the stairs ended.

Creak. I climb some more.

I can see her, standing in the doorway of a bedroom, beckoning to me, summoning me to her. I feel my arm rising, my hand starts to reach to her, I can see her. She's there, right there.

I lift my foot to the next step. There is no creak. There is no step. I watch the horizon as it arcs past my eyes. The rubble on the ground fills my vision. I have just a second to gasp before blackness sets in.

Lights. Blue, flashing lights.

I hear my mother's voice.

"I thought he was a bit depressed, but I never thought he would..."

"Calm yourself now, Mary, let's get him to hospital and see what's what." My dad offers his usual practical advice.

"Can you open your eyes?" It's a stranger's voice, I want to say *No, I can't* but the words don't come. In the blackness, I see a pale patch. It's growing. No. No, it's coming towards me. It's a face. It's her face.

"Come on, you never did try new things did you?" She reaches her hand out to me. I reach out and take it.

I'm tired of memories. I am going to try new things.

**The Festival of Nets**

**Part Two: The Closing Net**

**By Sean Patrick Giblin**

Stepping out from the gloom laden interior of the Narrow Staircase's upper windows, Demen felt the cold caress of the wind bite at his exposed skin. The mottled blotches and ripples that covered his greying flesh swam against the night and shifted and writhed in order to keep him enclosed in the shadows as the Fisher's sickle light waxed and waned with the crossing of scuttling clouds. All he wore was a pair of soft rubber foot pads strapped to his feet, and a tightly bound loin cloth that wrapped and cupped his woman-pleaser and companions with both a firm and secure discomfort. A little discomfort however, he reminded himself, was far preferable to the unexpected closing of an open window upon a poor, unsuspecting naked thief.

Demen slowly shifted himself along the thin stone lintel. He found the gutter pipe at the edge of the building, a solid and thickly rusted tube that kept the roof from flooding. As long as it was cleaned out, of course, and judging from the collection of mulch and pigeon nests gathered about the chute, he guessed that that was very rarely.

Reaching the ground and landing in a sludgy collection of refuse and detritus, he was unable to suppress a grin of satisfaction as his eyes lit upon the unguarded courtyard of the temple. Mottled shadows played across his skin, obscuring his appearance from wandering eyes. He darted across the courtyard and paused when he came to the blood-stained stone altar. The body of the crippled thief still lay there, headless and chopped to pieces.

He heard a half-human howl from somewhere off in the distance. The Thief Catchers had descended upon the city with all the zeal of ravenous wolves closing in upon a startled hare. He, however, was about to walk straight into the wolves very den beneath their slathering noses, and this thought alone spurred him onwards. He moved from shadow to shadow like a shade, his skin changing tone and pitch to match the light and colour of his surroundings as he went. It was not easy to maintain this sort of concentration. It had taken years to perfect, and there had been a time when he had not been able to control it at all.

Dangerous days, those had been, especially with the Horogomy closing its grip on his home island of Mord. Changeling's no longer had the mild freedom they'd enjoyed before the Horogomy came. His home was now plagued by the witch-hunters and Judges of the Ministry. Here on the Isle of Bereft, they didn't have Changelings. They had the Cursed. Men and women possessed of some other form of sorcery, a cousin to the Changeling arts, though Demen had never met one of these Cursed himself, he'd heard plenty of stories about how they were treated here in the Horogomy.

He reached the edge of the temple walls; there was a stone shelf that wound its way around the wall and was spiked at even intervals a hand span apart from one another. A keen warning to stay out, but not a deterrent from entering that was for sure. These Thief Catchers were arrogant bastards. The thought that anyone would dare to tread upon their sacred ground did not seem to cross their twisted minds. He leapt at the wall and propelled himself upward, catching the ledge with the tips of his fingers. His skin changed from mottled shadow to a dark metallic shimmer to match the metal plating which covered the stone walls at the top edge. With a grunt, he pulled himself up and then over onto the other side.

He landed on cool, wet grass and crawling on all fours, made his way across the overgrown lawn and onto the gravelled path that led to the temple. It took him a few minutes of searching before he found a window that would be inclined to his nimble fingers. Just like his employer back in Rest had told him, the windows had not been replaced since it had been a brewery, which meant that they had not been made to keep thieves out and that they were old. Both of which would play into his hands nicely.

It wasn't long before he had the large window open and had slipped inside. A few azure-flamed alchemical gas-lights lit up the corridors and stairwells and left plenty of shadowed pockets for him to take refuge in. This was going to be too easy. Thick carpets of purple and cream, stylized with a matrix pattern of eyes and claws ran along the length of the corridors, muffling his foot falls. He made his way up to the first floor and came out upon a wide balcony walkway that overlooked the unlit ground floor lobby. There were eight stairwells winding their way up to the floor he was on from all directions. The place was eerily silent, not a good omen in his book.

He was starting to get a bad feeling; it was like an itch that couldn't be scratched, like a worm burrowing beneath his skin. He shook it off. What was he worrying for? All the priests were out. His employer had told him that the place would be virtually empty. Still this did little to dissuade his years of criminal-honed instincts that had kept him alive on the violent streets of Rest, from buzzing like a kicked hornets' nest.

He heard footsteps. An orange light spilled out across the moonlit marble tiles of the ground floor lobby, followed by two voices. One female, the other male.

"It's not fair I tell you," the man complained. "It just bloody well isn't!"

"Quit your whining Nef. You don't hear me whinging do you?"

"Well no, but that's cause you haven't been here as long as I have, Dowel."

From between the balcony banisters Demen watched as two acolytes in long, flowing, dark purple cloaks, belted at the waist, strode into the lobby. The woman held an orange-lit alchemical globe in one hand, the fiery smoke curling out from her hands. He moved slowly on the upper floor, matching the stride of the two guards as they moved below.

"So what? That just means you've fucked up more than I have."

"But like I said, it's not fair. It wasn't my fault. It was that damn Regan and his - "

"What part of I don't give a fuck don't you're pea sized brain get?" The woman named Dowel strode ahead of the man named Nef, obviously tired of this argument. Demen came to a twisting staircase and leapt the banister, landing silently on the carpeted stairs.

"Ah, I'm sorry Dowel. It's just I wish I was out there you know. Chasing down the thieves and slitting me some Hag cursed throats." They both stopped then and Dowel turned to face Nef. Demen slowed his breathing. He was now only feet away from the two sentries, and the woman's gas-light was just caressing the edge of his shadows. Faint orange ripples drifted lightly across his bare skin.

"Don't we all? But here we are stuck watching the kids instead," said Dowel, turning and striding across the lobby of black and white tiles once more, her feet clacking against the polished marble.

"What kids?" Nef called after her.

"It's just an expression you fat turd."

"Oh. Good one."

"Huh. Come on, let's do another round."

"Can we visit that secret place of yours again?" Nef grabbed Dowel's behind. She turned and swatted his hand away, but playfully. Demen who had started to come up behind the man, quickly rolled to the side as the gas-light turned upon his position.

"Depends," Dowel said with mock sincerity.

"On what?"

"Whether or not I find anything larger than that cockroach you have renting the space above your balls before we get there."

"Ah, that hurts, Dowel."

"It's supposed to, love."

The two acolytes moved on, the orange glow of ghostly finger trails disappearing as they went further away, and then left the lobby through a tall set of oak doors that must have led to a library judging by the flash of scrolls Demen got as the woman's light touched upon its interior. The door closed and once again Demen found himself alone with only the faint glow of the Fisher to guide him. This was almost too easy. If that was all the patrol he was going to have to face, he may as well have left his clothes on and done this as a regular sneak thief. His talents were being wasted here. Still, the night was far from over.

He moved on through the lower floors of the temple, drifting from gloom laden corridor to gloom laden corridor. From what his employer had told him, the entrance to the vaults crypt would be at the back of the building. The vaults upper levels were where the brewing vats had once been kept. He found the entrance to the vaults and opening the heavy, rounded door, he was assailed by the stench of old wheat and rats piss. He passed through dusty and cobwebbed-festooned walkways lined with old rusted brewing tanks, and came across many broken barrels as well. The further he went in the more the place reeked and the floors were sticky and dark.

When he found the entrance to the lower vault, the place which had been built even before the city, he was surprised to see that his employer had been telling the truth. The entrance looked like some fairy-tale entrance into the abyss. There was no door, but rather a grand arch fashioned in the style of bony clawing hands. The darkness from the depths was cold; he saw his breath fogging before eyes.

Shit. He really wished he had brought some clothes with him. If only his gifts included camouflage from the cold. As he stepped into the grasping darkness the chill flooded into him, freezing him to the bone. Damn but his employer hadn't told him about this part. Not for the first time, he prayed to the Fisher and the Crooked Three that this was all going to be worth it in the end.

He walked down and down further into darkness, for some time. His night vision kicked in about fifteen minutes into his descent. That was when he saw the pale light of distant illuminations far below. The stairs had opened out into a wide chamber of stone, a grand cavern deep beneath the city, and the stone steps wound around the outside of the chamber like a snake coiled around an egg.

At the very bottom of the chamber he saw the source of the pale light. It emanated from a stone plinth in the centre of a clear space. Upon the raised block of stone lay a Claw, much like the one that had been attached to the Judge's arm, except this one was made of gold and laced with silver. Demen's skin glistened in the silvery light as he came upon the stone plinth. If watchers had been in place they would only have seen the slightest of ripples as he moved low across the ground.

He reached the plinth and rose to his feet, looking down at the Claw. It was a Reavers Claw. Three symbols there were of a Reaver. His iron mask, his blue cracking sword and the ornate Claw that was said to give the Reaver his personality or enhanced it or some such thing. Demen wasn't much of an expert on the matter. His skills with the Reavers lay specifically with avoiding the bastards at all costs.

But he did know one thing, and that was that their Claws were said to be masterful works of alchemical, artificial engineering and craftsmanship, designed by the Watcher himself when he had stepped forth from Donnardriss over a thousand years ago. So he had no illusions as to the value of this artefact. Still, he felt uneasy touching such a vile thing. Not for the first time he wished he could have been there the day the Watcher stepped out from the doorless city of the Cier, so that he could have kicked his ass right back over those walls.

He reached out a hand and was surprised to see that his skin lost its usual mottled shade as it came close to the Claw, looking almost as normal as a regular person's. He hesitated for a second, but before he could touch the artefact he felt that familiar and well worn feeling of eyes upon him and spun about.

In all the longs years since he had mastered his Change, he had never once let his emotions take control again. When he saw who was watching him however, the sea of calm that kept his skin in his control got a little choppy. Waves and shades rippled over him, and he could not claw back the concentration he needed to assert control. The fear was too great and it only grew.

The first Reaver stepped forward from the shadows and was soon joined by two more, their iron masks three dark slits beneath deep, crimson cowls, identical in their fierce scrutiny. Each wore a claw upon their left arm, and each Claw was unique in style and design. Of their blue-wreathed blades, he could see no sign, not that they needed them against him. The three Reaver's stepped in mockery of one another, like shades from some Coreseni vengeance play. Demen felt a warm stream trail its way down his leg and suppressed a crazed chuckle.

"Look what we have here, brother," said a snakelike and feminine voice from behind one of the masks. "A Changeling thief."

"He has soiled himself as well," another, the tallest of the three said with equal disgust and amusement.

The one in the centre took an extra step forward as the other two halted a few feet from Demen. "Thrice sinned," he said, sounding neither pleased nor disappointed, which almost made Demen's legs, give way beneath him.

"Retrieve Silverfrost," the lead Reaver then said haughtily, taking his gaze from Demen and surveying the surrounding chamber with mocking curiosity.

Demen found his fear giving way to anger at the indifference this bastard was showing for him. It was almost as if Demen wasn't going anywhere as far as he was concerned, so there was no reason for him to be a bother for them any longer. Well, fuck that. Demen reached out, taking the Claw, and tossed it in the face of the lead Reaver. The man moved like a serpent and snatched the Claw out of the air with such speed it was in the Reaver's hand before Demen even registered it.

"Shit," Demen hissed, and then he turned and ran.

"Retrieve the Changeling," he heard the Reaver leader say evenly.

Demen headed for the stairs, back the way he had come.

"He's a hard one to track," a voice said from beside him. He turned his head to look for the source of the voice but found only silver laced darkness and cold stone.

"But very noisy," said a heavier voice from in front of him. He turned in time to see the largest of the three Reavers standing before the stairs. A hand like a sledgehammer cracked against the side of Demen's head and sent him sprawling in a heap back the way he had just ran.

Head spinning he looked up to find three blurry masks looking down on him.

"I imagine that you thought your cursed abilities would keep you safe forever. You were wrong. The Eye of the Watcher is ever searching for your kind and nothing you do will ever hide you from His justice."

Something pricked him on the side of the neck. He reached a hand to feel for a wound and found nothing. That was when he caught the tone of his skin in wan silver light. The mottled grey washed away from his skin and for the first time in his life naked to the world, Demen Hash was revealed for the miserable, pot-bellied and crooked-nosed thief that he was. A fist came down along the back of his head and darkness swallowed him.

# HANUUT'S STAND

## BY NYKI BLATCHLEY

The city of Naamid burnt around Hanuut as he stormed the guard-post with his fellow-rebels. Soldiers of the Demon Queen held the broken gateway, ferocious at bay.

Hanuut didn't underestimate them. He'd served unwillingly in their ranks, hating the tyranny but seeing no way out. Like so many others, he'd taken his chance at last to join the rising as the liberating army of the Free Alliance approached the city's gate. He knew from his own training that these were formidable fighters.

His comrades were falling before the swords that defended the gate, but there was another way in. Sheathing the old, notched sword he'd grabbed before deserting, Hanuut reached up for a handhold on the rough stone wall and began to climb.

He was two storeys up when a warning shout from below cut through the din. He just had time to look up before a lump of masonry half his size came tumbling down on him, sweeping him off the wall. The impact on the ground knocked all the breath from him; but it seemed an infinitely long time before the stone crashed onto his leg. Searing pain filled him, and...

"They're coming!"

The shout jerked Hanuut from the nightmare of that terrible night — was it really only two nights ago?  He hauled himself into a sitting position, cursing the pain the movement sent through his half-healed stump, all they'd saved of his shattered leg.   The makeshift hospital where they'd brought him — a half-burnt inn, from the look of it — was crowded with the injured and dying on pallets and heavy with the stench of death.

He'd no doubt who *they* were, and he saw at a glance that no-one here was capable of resisting them.  Of the fighting-men, few were even conscious, let alone able to lift a weapon.

The wise-women who tended the sick, along with their younger apprentices, cowered in terror at what was coming. Hanuut found himself wishing, despite everything he'd never questioned, that the women here in Naamid were like those in Ario-ne to the north, who fought alongside the men.  These untrained women might have the courage to die shielding the sick and the children with their bodies, but that was all they could do.  They'd die and achieve nothing.

"How close are they?" Hanuut demanded.  Until today, the roar of his voice would have filled the room, but now his hoarse wheeze made him wince in pain at the effort.

A child stared at him with huge dark eyes. "They're coming up the street, sir." Her voice was soft with terror. "Are we going to be sacrificed to the Queen?"

"Not if I can help it," snapped Hanuut, though it was unlikely the remnants of the Imperial forces had anything that formal in mind. Looking at the little girl, he shuddered at visions of her fate.

He hesitated an instant, protesting silently that a man with one leg couldn't be expected to fight. That wasn't the point, though. Even if he tried to hide, it would do no good. He'd be cut down, in his bed or out of it. That was really the only choice to make.

"Find my sword," he told the child. "It's probably somewhere near the bed." She goggled at him. "Now would be a good time," he added, making an effort to be gentle with her.

As the girl scurried to search, Hanuut summoned the effort to raise his voice. "Someone get me up and strap me to the doorpost." Met by uncomprehending stares, he launched into a string of curses that brought shocked looks to the healers' faces, though one or two of the wide-eyed children seemed to be memorising the phrases he used.

"You can't," protested one of the healers, an old woman with a crumpled face. "You've lost a lot of blood, and the wound hasn't healed. You'll..."

"I'll die standing instead of lying down," he snapped. "Want to argue till they come. Now, get me up, or so help me, I'll take a sword to you myself."

There was a shocked exchange of glances, then two of the younger women came and hauled him up on either side, half helping and half carrying him to the door, where others waited with bandages. They wound the strips round the shattered doorframe — the door itself had clearly been splintered down in the fighting — and about his chest and waist, securing him in place, before retreating into the room. The child handed him the battered, notched sword, her face grave and scared.

Hanuut peered around the doorframe into what was left of the street. The building opposite — a petty merchant's establishment, by the look of it — was on fire, and several neighbouring structures were charred remains. The smoke-heavy air fixed islands of screams and yells amid an ocean of eerie silence. Two dozen paces away, a group lurched towards him, the rabble into which the proudest army might descend. Hanuut's last hope — that these were rebels, or the liberating forces — vanished at the sight of the Demon Queen's red flower emblazoning their torn surcoats.

The leader stopped two sword-lengths away, and the

surprise on his brutish, scarred face — a mahogany face, lighter than the people of Naamid — gave way quickly to mockery. "What do we have here?" he demanded. "They're giving us target practice now?"

An ugly laugh spread through the group. They knew — it must be true, Hanuut thought — that they'd be dead by sunset. The imperial garrison's last footholds were being overwhelmed, and there was no escaping the vengeance of the people they'd oppressed. They were as good as dead, but they were going out on a tide of blood and rape. They had nothing to lose — but nor did he, really, Hanuut reflected, as he felt the aching emptiness where his right leg used to be.

"You're not getting past me," he snarled, hoping his certainty could make it so.

"Oh no?" The man lunged at Hanuut, bloodshot eyes glaring with the lust to kill. In the heartbeat he had, Hanuut smelt the stench of drink on his breath and knew it gave him the advantage. Flicking the blade aside, he plunged his sword-point into the enemy's exposed breast, pushing it deep and then yanking it out with the suck of blood.

Another, the drunkest of the group, rushed at Hanuut yelling furiously, sword raised high. An easy target as it was, paying no attention to defence, the man stumbled onto the blood-soaked blade of his own accord.

After that, the survivors took more care. Doomed they might be, but they wanted to enjoy their orgy of slaughter for as long as possible, and they approached Hanuut with caution. Like most soldiers, they had little skill with the sword — in battle, a clumsy blow could kill you just as surely as a subtle thrust — but they didn't need it.

They tried to surround him, but the doorway prevented it. Hanuut, his head swimming with pain from his stump, tried to concentrate on countering each swipe or thrust and managed to get in a couple of wounding ripostes, but he was slowing down.

A searing agony cut through his guts, and he looked down stupidly at the blade he'd missed sticking out of his belly. As a mist rose in his eyes, another sword sliced deep into his shoulder. Hanuut sagged against the bindings. This was the end.

The yells of triumph turned to screams. His eyes cleared enough to see men striking at his attackers, and Hanuut recognised, with a lurch of relief, the insignia of the Alliance.

Then everything dissolved around him, and there was only a tunnel of light ahead of Hanuut.

# My Enemy Hands

## By Lynette Bishop

What kind of life is there left for a warrior who can no longer stand the sight of blood? That is the question.

I look at my hands in this frozen moment of time while the battle rages around me. Enemies, that's what they have become, these hands of mine. The body I am kneeling next to tells me that.

A movement behind me, the swish of a sword, register like a voice calling faintly from a distant land. I sweep my sword backwards, feel the jolt of impact on my arm as I thrust upwards and hear the scream of agony.

I'm good. Oh yes, I'm good. I could fight twenty men, thirty maybe, in the dark, leave no soul alive and afterwards feel nothing.

And yet there is this body.

I sense something and bend my head. An arrow speeds across the deadly space I leave and hits someone. I don't look up to see. I only hear, from that far land, the scream. I am still captured in this frozen moment.

It should not be lying here, this body. Jothan, my heart's brother. I feel the splintering, the tremor of grief as it unfreezes somewhere deep in my being. But I must not grieve. One hand, one of my enemy hands, reaches out to touch his face. I get quickly to my feet. My sword swings, parries, darts. I hear the screams but the pain of each fatal thrust pierces my own heart.

"Denedr."

I hear Erlart call my name but I do not turn.

"Where are you going?"

Night. I am in a cave in the Dark Mountains, crouching to the warmth of a small fire. Behind me shadows whisper of what I have done.

'You killed him.'

'You had to do it.'

'You left the battle.'

'It was all but over. Erlart could do what was left to do.'

'You have blood on your hands.'

'Of course. A warrior always has blood on his hands.'

'It is the blood of your closest friend.'

'It is the blood of a friend turned traitor.'

"No!"

I put my hands over my ears and rock back and forth. I cannot get the pain out of my heart. I cannot get the pictures out of my head. His eyes smiling, mocking, his sword at my throat. My stunned disbelief; undeniable truth tearing through me, breaking me and the anger, blood-red, consuming me. And finally, the body at my feet.

I stretch my hands out to the fire. If I plunge them in, will the price be paid?

"Denedr."

I am instantly on my feet, sword in my hand, but if this had been an enemy, I would be a dead man now. I drop the sword and sit. "Erlart," I say, "so you found me."

We sit in silence till I manage a question. "It's over then?"

He nods, solemn as he studies my face.

"The men are celebrating?" I ask.

"Yes. They fought well. You think they shouldn't celebrate?"

"Of course they should." I get up and go to the mouth of the cave. It's a clear night, cold. "I just wish..." But I don't have words. I look out across the stars above the impenetrable dark of the forests and lowlands and feel how small we are, Erlart and I. Jothan too, wherever he is now. Maybe in some after life where he is forgiven...

I look at my moon-bathed hands, my enemy hands, and wonder if I can ever forgive myself.

"You had to do it," says Erlart at my shoulder. "We have to keep on trying to stop them or there will never be an end to injustice and cruelty. The suffering will just go on and on. Unless another way, without bloodshed, is found to bring them down, this is what we must do. Let him go."

He's right, but you can't kill love as easily as you can kill a man.

The light is sudden, dazzling. I raise my hands to shield my eyes. A star. I have never seen its like in my life. Its white-gold heart burns with hints of all the colours beneath the sun. I can see this more clearly as it comes closer. I feel Erlart grip my shoulder as light fills our cave.

Then it is gone. Leaving a fading trail of brightness, it crests the Dark Mountains overhead. It is only when the last of its lingering light flickers out I see something that almost stops my heart.

"What the...?" begins Erlart. He is looking wide-eyed at my hands. They are glowing. Yes, glowing.

It is impossible to understand what has just happened so we do not even try to talk about it. The glow, lasting a second or two, no more, shines steadily on warm like sunlight in my mind and probably in Erlart's too. After a while we exchange a smile.

"Let's go and join the men," I say.

# Estampiel

## By Sandra Norval

It was a Wednesday. Estampiel rummaged through the pile of magazines and picked up a dog-eared copy of Modern Herald. Its glossy cover had seen much better days and stirred thoughts of how this seemed to represent his own life.

Flicking through the pages, he lingered over articles and short pieces. Articles like 'Exercise your inner Angel, Exorcise your inner Demon'. He snorted as he noted that the article had been written by his former intern, Comprael, now Guardian Angel of the IT worker. He wouldn't have minded, but the phrase in the title had been his training catchphrase. Typical.

Estampiel tossed the magazine back on the coffee table, where it slapped to its rest. He stood, arched his back, stretching out his muscles, then shrugged his cassock off his shoulders. The pages of the magazine flapped around in the breeze as his huge, white wings unfurled. He shook them out, a few feathers drifting away on the breeze he'd created. The wings dropped and hung, looking like rejected bedsheets, and, let's be honest here, they were just as yellowed.

The ticking of the clock seemed to keep getting louder and was just too irritating. With a grind, Estampiel pulled a chair across the room, placed it beneath the clock and clambered up. As the clock came away from the wall, a flurry of dust swirled around and landed in his nostrils. A sneeze soon dealt with that, splattering it across the plastic face of the clock. With a sniff, he swiped his sleeve across it and flipped it over to remove the batteries. The ticking ceased. Estampiel jumped off the chair and dropped the clock on top of the magazine. That was when he noticed the grey smudge across his sleeve. Tutting, he folded his wings, put his cassock back on his shoulders and dropped down onto the nearest chair.

The door swung open, and St Peter strolled in.

"Hey, Estampiel! How's philately going, making its stamp on the world?" He grinned and chuckled as he signed in. He clocked the clock on the table and frowned. With a sigh he slipped behind the counter and started scrabbling around in a drawer, mumbling "Batteries, batteries…"

Estampiel shifted in his seat, turned his back on Peter and folded his arms tightly across his chest.

Peter pulled out the batteries and sorted out the clock. He dusted the clock down with a yellow cloth from the drawer and rehung it. Tick, tick, tick, tick.

Estampiel rolled his eyes up to the ceiling and let out a long, slow breath.

"Met a friend of yours today," Peter said as he sauntered to the chair opposite Estampiel. "Roger Beswell."

Pain seared through his palms as the name registered in his mind. Roger Beswell. The last philatelist. If Peter had met him, it only meant one thing.

"Apparently, he died alone in his flat. His stamps were all around him. One last look, he said. Shame, really, guess that makes you redundant, doesn't it? Can't be a Guardian Angel with no-one left to guard."

The door opened again, and Maureen from Angel Resources walked in.

"Estampiel, come through."

"Happy retirement!" Peter shouted as the door clicked shut.

The chair released a puff of air as Estampiel lowered himself into it, and he cleared his throat to ease his embarrassment.

Maureen smiled sweetly, almost sympathetically, and he prepared himself for the immortal words 'I'm sorry but your role is redundant.'

"I'm sorry," she began, "to hear about Roger. You were very fond of him, weren't you?"

Estampiel nodded, bracing himself for the rest.

"Well, now he's joined us here, your role is redundant." His shoulders sagged. "But don't worry, that's a good thing." He snorted.

"No, really, it is a good thing because we've been in need of a new Guardian Angel. It's street dancers, you see. There's been a massive population explosion of street dancers, and they need all the help they can get. I mean, have you seen the way they throw themselves around?"

He couldn't stop himself from grinning now.

"Do you think they'll show me some moves?" he said.

"With your wings? I should think you'll be showing them a thing or two!" Maureen winked at him and handed over a parcel of all the things he'd need to know.

# Flame Dance

## By David Trebus

I was standing on the cliff top again. I always liked to stand there. It gave me a sense of control, as if the world beneath me were between my hands and mine to shape. The reality was always much less predictable. Today was no exception, as I stood there, the wind blowing through my hair. The moment I had been dreading, the moment I could never have planned for, had come.

Below me, a darkness spread over the land, creeping forward like a rolling wave washing into the bay. The scale of it was too much for my mind to comprehend, knowing that darkness was made up of thousands of people, all of them with their own hopes and dreams, fears and desires. But it was only one of them I was standing here waiting for.

I kneeled on the ground, bleached white armour glowing red in the dying light of the evening sun. I placed my hands to my chest and looked up at the sky, closing my eyes in  silent moments I knew couldn't last much longer.

"If you can hear me up there, I only have one wish on this night. One request to you on high, who have seen fit to put me in this place at this time. I beg of you, let me reach her, let me somehow get through to her, so I can save my land, my people...save her soul." I paused, a single tear rolling down my face as I opened my eyes.

"Take whatever you want, I don't care, just please help me save her, damnit!" I yelled at the sky, to the gods in my desperate hour, knowing that it was up to me and they couldn't help even if they wanted to.

At the same moment, a glint of light shone in the darkness, shining crystal blue in the sea of black. I knew instantly it was her, just as I knew she could see me standing up here, a halo of fire behind my head cast by the waning sun. The night was her power, though, which was why she had chosen this moment to come. But I knew, as long as I hoped and the fire burned within me, I could get through to her.

I took one last glance behind me, feeling that it could be the very last time I saw my sleepy little town, Aratha. It was sitting up there, sleepily preparing for night. They didn't know what was coming, and, if I had anything to say about it, they never would. I would protect them until my very last breath, or die trying.

I turned and took a few steps back towards Aratha. My feet wanted me to keep walking, just run away from the dark tide sweeping towards me. I shut my eyes again and turned my thoughts inwards, steeling myself for what I had to do. It was time. No more running, no more hesitating.

I turned again, walking towards the cliff edge. I began to jog, then broke into a run. I reached the edge and leapt into the air, falling towards the darkness below me, straight towards the roiling black. Fire leapt at my back as two giant flames erupted from my shoulder-blades. The flames formed into wings of crimson fire behind me, catching the wind and propelling me forward even faster.

The light from my flames illuminated some of the host arrayed beneath me. Warriors all of them, men and women, clad not in black but in darkest blue like deep ocean, each one of them summoned by the will of my lover's master to take away everything that I held dear in the world. They weren't my objective; I would only fight them if I had to. To stop this madness I had to find her, I had to stop her, or it would go on forever.

Arrows began to fly towards me from the ground, but they had no chance of touching me. They burst into flames, turning into harmless ash by the time they reached my armour, staining it grey. I turned my path towards where the blue light had shone from the head of the advancing host, aiming to end this quickly.

Bright blue light erupted from the darkness below as two wings, matching my own but of blue fire, sprang up. A chill spread through the air around me, threatening to smother my flames in the deathly cold. My breath began to mist and my flames shrink as waves of cold assaulted me.

Smiling, I knew she was trying to scare me off. Even after what her master had done to her, deep down a part of her still didn't want to face me, to confront me and the past I represented. Her past. She had always been one to run from her problems rather than face them—a bit like me, really.

The fires of my soul were never so easy to put out, however, and as I thought of all the moments we had shared, the love we had shared, the fires sprang up all over again. my wings burnt brighter and larger than I had ever felt before, even at my ascension months before. I kept on, forcing her to confront me, my will set on the path I had to take.

I reached the ground , my wings of flame turning downwards to slow my descent, scorching the ground around me as I landed before her at the foot of the cliff. It was at the small entrance that led up to my home, blocking the path they had to take to quell the ancient flame that lay within.

"Hello, Eldiri. You know I can't let you past this point," I said as she strode forward to face me, the cold of her blue flames frosting the grass white as she walked.

"Hello, Ven. I knew you would come my, love, just as I'm sure you know I won't change my mind. All these people around me need their home just as much as yours need theirs"

"That's him talking. We don't need to fight each other, if we just…" She cut me off with a wave of her hand.

"Don't be so naïve. I took the cold inside me to save them. He can say what he wants, his cold touch made me sick, just as your warm touch always melted my heart. But I'm afraid now nothing can save me. At least I can save my people by doing this. Please, Ven, get out of my way, I don't want to fight you."

"No chance. If I have to burn away what he's done to save you and my people, then that's what I'll do. I'll try not to hurt any of your soldiers in the process."

"You stubborn bastard, Ven. Fine, if I have to snuff out your fire, then so be it!" Eldiri yelled. Perfectly formed ice crystals fell from her eyes to shatter on the ground.

She launched herself towards me, her wings of blue flame alight with spectral energy. She drew her sword, casting it through her wings. It seemed to catch the blue light, even as the blade turned ice blue and blue flames began to dance along it.

I barely had time to form my own blade of fire before she was right in front of me, aiming a cut at my neck. It manifested in my hand, leaping to life, born from my love for Eldiri and my desire to protect those closest to me. I just hoped it would be enough to burn away the cold she had taken into herself.

Fire and ice met in a clash of blinding light. If the gods on high had not heard my prayers, then they would at least see the desperate struggle unfolding beneath them. If nothing else could move them to take action, then maybe this would: two primal forces meeting, two lovers fighting in a sea of dark-blue night.

Our blades clashed again and again as we danced the deadly duet of battle. I could see her bright blue eyes shining at me, still shedding tears of ice which evaporated from the flames of my wings. She stared back at me, into my eyes — red eyes, the consequence of me taking in the sacred fire — and I knew a battle was being waged inside her soul while we fought.

We leapt back at the same moment, sweat streaking down my face, breath misting heavily before hers. I lowered my blade, mirroring her actions as she stood before me. Her wings shrank and dulled as the ice of her heart began to melt. My flames only grew stronger as I knew I was getting through to her, I was reaching her — I dared to hope.

I smiled at her, but Eldiri's face turned to one of horror as she looked at me. She started to run towards me, but my vision blurred. I felt pain and looked down to see its source. A sword tip of ice met my swimming vision before it vanished, pulled out by its wielder. My wings of flame faded, shrinking, as my consciousness slipped away. Someone whispered into my ear, "She's mine now, Ven. Your town, your fire, your love: they are all mine. Think on that as I leave your flame to slowly fade to an ember in the night."

I fell to the ground, and my sword of flame vanished. I felt suddenly cold and couldn't help shivering. The last thing I saw that night was Eldiri running towards me, her flames of blue burning bright as tears of ice streamed behind her.

# I SEE A VOICE

## BY NYKI BLATCHLEY

"Are you two awake?"

"That supposed to be a joke?  You know I haven't slept in a thousand years."

"I'm sorry, I couldn't resist.  And how about you?"

"Um... oh, yes, yes, yes, I'm awake.  Of course I am.  What's going on now?"

"I think we have another one coming."

"And you know that how?"

"I just went to the entrance.  She was standing outside, obviously building up to coming in."

"She?  Well, I never.  It's not very often we get the fair sex, is it?"

"Right.  No point coming here if you can't fight."

"Oh yes?  Are you suggesting we can't fight?  I came closer to killing the Beast than either of you *men*."

"Oh... sorry, forgot. Not easy to remember, in the circumstances."

"Oh, I wouldn't say that. No, not at all."

"Quiet. Here she comes. She should be making her challenge about now."

"Hear me, foul beast! I, Tiriana, Warrior Princess of the Shandalan Empire, have sworn a solemn oath to end your reign of evil. Here I stand, ready to slay you in single combat. Answer me, loathly creature, or be known as a craven forever!"

"Upon my word, she did that well, did she not?"

"Heard better. Warrior Princess? She looks so young."

"Well, you can be a princess at any age, can't you?"

"I know that. Thinking more about the warrior part."

"She's very pretty, anyway. Beauteously fair."

"And just what's that got to do with fighting the Beast?"

"Well... nothing. I was merely endeavouring to say..."

"You're always endeavouring to say."

"I am a philosopher and poet, don't you know? Is it not natural that I should contemplate beauty?"

115

"Well, contemplate away, but you wouldn't stand a chance with her, even if you were corporeal."

"Especially if he were corporeal, I'd say. Any case, if the Beast kills her, she'll be caught in the magical field like the rest of us. Be here for eternity."

"To be sure, but she'll be incorporeal. I shall not be able to gaze on her fair form."

"Quiet. I think she's going to speak again."

"I call upon you a second time, foul beast! If you will not face me in combat, I claim all that is yours, to the glory of the Shandalan Empire."

"What's this Shandalan Empire? Never heard of it."

"Oh, I don't know. These kingdoms and empires come and go so fast it can make you dizzy. I don't think it was around five hundred years ago."

"What was that old empire? Let me see, let me see... You know, the big one."

"Oh, right. As opposed to a small empire?"

"Oh, you know what I mean, to be sure. It was a *very* big empire. A fair empress ruled there, and she had a gorgeous pair of…"

"Oh, really.  Can't you think of anything else?"

"Eyes, I was going to say.  Yes, yes.  She had big, blue eyes.
She was an exceedingly pretty girl."

"I think you mean the Mellovu Empire.  That was thousands
of years ago, and it lasted barely a century.  You wouldn't have
remembered if it had been ruled by a man, would you?"

"I dare say I wouldn't, but the beauty of a fair woman
remains in the heart of a poet."

"If you like a girl who wears her enemies' shrunken heads
around her neck.  Anyway, what's this got to do with anything?"

"Er… I can't remember.  I'm sure it was relevant, though."

"What's the Beast doing?  Can't see from here?"

"I can see it, but I think it's waiting for the third challenge.
You know what a stickler for tradition it's always been."

"Lass is getting nervous."

"Oh, come now, come now.  Considering that she may be
about to die in glorious combat, you might do her the honour of
calling her a Warrior Princess."

"I call on you for one last time, beast!  I name you coward!  Unless you stand before me now, I shall hold you up to ridicule before the entire world."

"Uh-oh, that's done it.  Here it comes."

"Oh, what a good move!  You know, this one might actually have a chance."

"I say, watch that tentacle, girl.  To say nothing of the other eleven."

"Must have hurt."

"Not when she's wearing armour like that.  She certainly knows how to use her sword."

"Great Shade's name, is she a warrior or a tumbler?"

"Oh, I sincerely hope she's both.  There she goes again.  What a wonderful black-flip that was, don't you think?"

"She's got it!  Maybe it's dead."

"Are you serious?  That just annoyed it.  Any time now..."

"Yes, here comes the flames from its snout.  Oh no, it's got the blue fire going.  I can't even see her.  She must be burnt to a frazzle."

"No, still on her feet. Hurt, though. Hair's definitely singed."

"What a pity. She has such pretty hair."

"Oh, be quiet. Can't you think about anything else?"

"What? I've never even mentioned her hair before. I was merely endeavouring to say..."

"She's down. No, I can't look. What's happening?"

"Beast's got its mouth open so far I can see its tonsils."

"Upon my word. Does the Beast really have tonsils?"

"I was using hyperbole. Don't you know anything?"

"I know everything there is to know about hyperbole. I used it all the time in my poetry. On one occasion..."

"No, look, she's up again. Yes, yes, yes..."

"Gone."

"No, she's still fighting inside its mouth, dodging its teeth. There, the Beast's crumpling. it's dead."

"Oh, I say, what happened?"

"I think she stabbed through to the brain from inside its

mouth. That's incredible."

"Is she still alive, by any chance?"

"Oh, please. You know how sharp those teeth are. The poor thing didn't have a hope."

"Where am I? What's going on? Who are you people?"

"Now, don't be scared, girl. We're not going to hurt you. Well, we can't in any case, but we wouldn't, even if we could."

"What? I was fighting the Beast and... What happened?"

"Technical term is a draw. You killed it, it killed you. So here you are."

"Where's here? And who are you?"

"We all came here to kill the Beast at one time or another, and our souls were caught in the magical field. Just like yours was. I'm afraid you're here for eternity."

"So, how many of you are there?"

"Hundreds, but most of them can't handle it. They go to sleep and don't wake. A couple have slept for ten thousand years. We're the only ones who stay awake. I hope you'll join us."

"You're really very pretty, you know, my dear. At least, you were."

"Just ignore him.  Now, tell us what's been going on in the world for the past couple of centuries."

## Song

### By David Trebus

Embrace your love, embrace your pain

Seek out that lonely island in the distance

Fight your fate, keep trying in vain

Looking out for that hope so elusive

Reach out for love, fight the pain

Seek out that lonely figure in the distance

Embrace your fear, your efforts not in vain

Looking out for that moment so fleeting

Feel  your love, move past the pain

Seek out that lonely moment in the distance

Fight your despair, hope never in vain

Looking out for that person so ephemeral.

# Story

## By David Trebus

It's not as if you have never walked a lonely path

It's not as if you have never spent a night in tears

Why is it you cannot perceive me today?

Why is it you won't let me show you the way?

This broken voice, with it I will shout until I am heard

These fractured words, with them I will write until they are read

These silent gestures, with them I will move until I am seen

These fragile emotions, with them I will reach out until I am embraced

It's not as if you haven't been hurt

It's not as if you haven't spent time in pain

Why is it I cannot seem to help?

Why is it I am always trying in vain?


This broken voice, with it I will shout until I am heard

These fractured words, with them I will write until they are read

These silent gestures, with them I will move until I am seen

These fragile emotions, with them I will reach out until I am embraced

# Turmoil
## By Sandra Norval

Emily sat at the table. Her fingers still tingled from the scrubbing, and the smell of caustic prickled her nostrils. It had taken hours to get the room clean; even now she couldn't be sure. Blood spots weren't that easy to see in candlelight. She took a deep rasping breath. She preferred the scent to the sticky, warm smell of old blood.

In all her years as a midwife, she'd never quite learnt to deal with the loss of a child. Each one meant the loss of a promise. A promise from the Gods that a life would be lived, a mark would be made. What mark was ever made by a dead baby?

She sighed and lifted her body from the chair, listening to her own footsteps, heavy, scraping across the bare wooden floor. As she passed the candle, she picked it up and made her way up the stairs to bed.

It was a fitful night of sleep. Even as she first closed her eyes, the images of lost infants swirled before her. She snapped her eyes open again, panting as the fear coursed through her. Every time it was this way. They came to claim the new spirit, to lead it to the other world. For her it was a comfort. Though she feared their presence, she liked to know that every child had a place, even if it wasn't in this world. She closed her eyes again and watched the spirits swirl and dissipate like smoke in a breeze. She dreamed that she was waving them off, and the fear gave way to a strange calm, the kind of calm that only came when a deal had been struck.

****

Twenty years had passed, countless babies were born and raised, but numerous little souls had been sent on their way to the other world. It made no difference how she handled each birth, Nature had her own ways of choosing which would live and which would not. And every one had ended with a visit from the spirit children, a final farewell as their spirits moved along.

When Margaret lost her child on that table, Emily knew that there was something different.

Margaret lay bleeding, screaming in agony even after the child had been taken and the cord severed. Her cries echoed around the valley, haunting Emily as she fetched more water from the well. As another scream rang out, she looked to the skies and was almost certain the veil of stars shifted as if recoiling with horror at the sound. All she could do was wait for the end that she knew would come.

Back inside, she refilled the kettle and set it back over the fire. She kept mopping the blood as best she could, but it was always replaced. With a fresh cloth she mopped Margaret's brow, chasing her head as she writhed with the pain.

"Shh, Margaret, shh. I'm here, do not be afraid."

Margaret reached for Emily's smock, twisted it between her fingers, pulling the midwife towards her. For just a split second her wails ceased, their eyes met and Emily waited. Margaret's eyes were wide and staring as she drew a sharp breath in, juddered, wailed one last time. As her life faded, the wail petered out to silence, and Emily tugged her smock from the dead woman's hand.

The dream started as always, with the spirit children swirling around, glimpses of little faces teasing her mind's eye. This time their little hands tugged at her, willing her to come, follow, join them. The times had taken their toll on her will, and she found herself drifting after them, down into the dark void below.

Into the darkness she floated, no longer sure which way was up and which way down; she allowed herself to drift, assuming that this was how it was to be.

But one should never assume.

As she waited, alone but calm, she saw tiny pinpricks of light begin to appear in the distance. Gradually they multiplied, and the veil of stars she had seen in the night sky so many times appeared before her. Slowly they began to swirl and swarm, taking the shape of some kind of being. A huge face filled the sky, both beautiful and frightening. Emily was unable to look away. He looked down upon her and spoke.

"Emily. We owe you a great debt. You have brought our children here where they could rest in peace." He waited, but her response stuck in her throat and she uttered no more than a few curious croaks. He looked away from her and sighed. Afraid she had disappointed him, she reached out a hand and stuttered, but still no sentence came.

His starry eyes turned to her again and she smiled, pleased to have a second chance.

"You have no children of your own," he said, "and these children have no mother. You will stay here, care for them, love and cherish them as if you gave them life yourself."

Suddenly she found her voice.

"No! No! No!" she cried, "I'm needed in my world!"

"This is your world now," he said, and the stars slid away, covered the sky, then faded away to darkness. The spirit babies swirled around, each grabbing at her, and she floated away with them.

Emily's house was burned to the ground when they found Margaret's bloody remains, but Emily and the stillborn child were missing.

****

It was the fifth anniversary of Margaret's death when Sarah felt the first twinge in her womb. No children had been delivered in the village since Emily disappeared. All the mothers had left to stay with relatives before they were confined. Sarah had left it too late.

Michael paced around the kitchen, helpless.

"You will have to do it. All you have to do is be ready to take it when it arrives." She winced and gritted her teeth as the next contraction took grip. Michael stood and stared, wanting to run but knowing there was no-one to run to. Sarah sighed and relaxed, the pain now gone.

Michael began pacing again, his footsteps loud on the wooden floor. He almost missed the knock at the door. Sarah looked up and nodded; surely an extra pair of hands would be a help.

He threw the bolt and peered out. On the verandah stood a hooded figure.

"You need my help." It was a woman's voice, and he was relieved. She took down the hood and he staggered backwards.

"E...Emily's here," he said and stepped aside to let her in.

It was then that he saw it: lit by the moon, her house had been restored.

He closed the door behind him, but it barely muffled the screams of his wife as he paced up and down outside.

A while later, the door opened and Emily stepped out, a tightly wrapped bundle in her arms. In silence she turned to him, face pale in the moonlight. She turned away and walked back to her house, carrying the bundle with her. As she closed the door behind her, a cloud slid across the moon and the building faded away, leaving just the scattered, charred remains.

The only sound Michael could hear was the bitter wail from his stricken wife.

# The Celebration of Seven

## By Lynette Bishop

The Carthamensas Circle begins with forest. That's where the vern-wolves live. Trees climb up sheer rock like they're trying to get out of a place where, when you hear howling, you know something's died. The sheer rock is the foot of the mountain that kicks you back into the forest. If you could get over the mountain, which by all accounts is impossible, you'd have a great view of sand. The sand is pale gold but it's called the Blue Desert. Being so far north, it never gets the sun. Some of this stuff they teach us at school, the boring bits. The other parts you hear first when you're a little kid and the big kids want to scare you. Soon you're picking up enough stories to keep you in nightmares for weeks to come.

The Circle has six rings. Circle's a misleading name. It doesn't go round the city. It's more like layers. Terracona, our neighbour across the plain and also facing north, claims a share of the Circle, though you have to say 'Terracona Circle' doesn't quite have the same ring to it. Anyway, their section of the Circle has the same six rings. The next ring is the Sea of Storms where, though again it's only what people say, waves freeze as they roll. After that, drifting into the Sea is our local slice of the Ice Pole. The last ring's the one people argue over. The opinion of optimists and dreamers is that it's Galsantos, the perfect city, but just as many people are sure it's the Void. Heaven or Hell, the stuff of legends.

The bottom line is that nobody knows for certain about any of it, the places or the creatures that eyewitness reports say live in them. How you can have eyewitnesses when nobody's been there, I don't know. No-one crosses the border of Carthamensas into the Outlands. Except, of course, the families with seven children, which don't count as they're only going to Camp Cheer and back. They're big news when the seventh baby's born. There's a street party and stuff like that, but you don't hear anything about them once they're gone. You don't know if they've seen anything of the Circle. Why would they though if they're going to Camp Cheer? And no-one wants to hear how great that is when only rich people like the Braga can afford to go.

I used to feel like that but now it's what we are, a family of seven kids, I feel different. I want to know that it really is great there. At the moment we're in the Outlands, driving through in a hired jeep-mobile. Compared to the city, which is blocks of buildings and squares of concrete, it has us wide-eyed. Meadow and woodland, it's a natural barrier between the city border and the first ring of the Circle. We're not going to the Circle but right now our jeep-mobile is coming over the brow of a hill and we're getting a view of the forest in the distance. I hope this is as close as we're going to get.

"Hey, dad! Turn round." I'm the oldest, fourteen and, being a boy, I feel it's up to me to try and bring things round if dad gets out of line. That's not too often, but now wouldn't be a good time to act a bit crazy like he has lately.

"Wow, is that the forest!" Jackro is twelve.

"I'm hungry." Vern's only three. There are also three sisters. One of them is pulling dad's sleeve to turn back. One's crying and one, believe it or not, is sleeping.

"Yeah, right," says dad. "Guess we took a wrong turn somewhere." He makes no move to turn the jeep-mobile round though.

When I say three sisters, I mean four. I suppose you should count Katy Kay even though she's only five days old. It is, after all, because of her we're getting this holiday. She's asleep too. Trixy, who's pulling at dad's sleeve, is holding her.

"Are we there now?" Vern again. He just doesn't get it. Does this look like Camp Cheer? What it looks like is the middle of nowhere and something about the road ahead, too straight, too perfect, doesn't seem right. Why is there a road into the forest at all?

"You ok, Vern?" asks dad. "Sure there'll be a turning soon." He keeps heading towards the forest.

All of us kids know the stories of the creatures of the Circle, and I can feel the younger ones tensing, even Jackro. What if there's no turning? Besides the vern-wolves there are blood scaratrixes in the forest. They're this giant worm kind of thing with fangs and suckers. Another scaratrix lives in the desert. But we're not worrying about that one yet, even though the sand scaratrix can freeze its prey or bury it alive in sand. At the moment three creatures are enough to have us sinking back into our seats as if we could propel the jeep-mobile backwards. The third creature that could be around here is the jacksaw roc, which cuts through the skies anywhere in the Circle and cuts through flesh and bone too, swooping and seizing in a split second anything that moves. That makes three good reasons for dad to turn back before we hit the forest.

Camp Cheer, as I said, is where we're heading. A whole week there free is a reward given to families who have managed to produce seven children. Why that is, I don't know. Tradition, they say. It's certainly not from the Braga who rule Carthamensas. They believe wholeheartedly in making life in the city as miserable as possible. For example, every street has its shops, school, leisure centre, things like that, but here's where you see how bad life is. There's a small law office and it's always closed, but the equally small medi-centre has to stay open twenty-four hours because it always has long queues outside.

Another thing that's bad is why the apartment buildings that make up the street are only fifty storeys high. This is because the Braga haven't got the manpower for more patrols. The fly-hovers sweep past regularly, checking from the third floor up, otherwise too many people jump. If you jump they take your family away, nobody knows where, but people who hurl themselves from their living room windows are past caring about anything except not having to live in Carthamensas anymore.

I think kids survive because there's always the dream of becoming one of seven and going to Camp Cheer. That must keep some parents going too. My dad told me once when he'd had too much poltrin to drink that some people even dream of getting away to Galsantos. I think he might be one of them and, if he is, that's a dangerous dream he carries because you might as well jump as try to get through the Circle. Even if there are no creatures there, there's something. I don't think you can reach the other side of it alive. I hope as we keep heading down this road towards the forest that he's not thinking of trying to get there now.

We're supposed to be protected. That's why you have to wait till there are seven children, each one named for one of the creatures of the Circle and each one carrying protection against all the monsters with his or her name. Why we need this when we're only going to Camp Cheer, I don't know. The camp is in the middle of a wood but we're talking small wood here, not forest. There are huts to sleep in, a grassy place to play and a small river running through it. Absolutely no danger.

"Dad, Scarly needs to pee."

Trixy's taken over since mom's not here, though she's only nine. There should have been a nursing help along to take care of Katy Kay, but dad said she couldn't come. Mom would have come if she wasn't so ill. She's got a week instead at this amazing place called the Spa Centre. That's in the Outlands too, but dad says it's not near where we're going.

I really thought mom would come with us till a few days ago, even though the Spa Centre's where all the seventh-baby moms go. When she came home with Katy Kay I could see she was too ill. She hugged us all when she came home, a tight hug that didn't feel quite right. She held Katy Kay the same way right up till they came to take her to the Spa. She cried so much the few days she was home, I could see she needed the break. Dad tried all the time to take Katy Kay to let her rest but she just screamed at him. They did a lot of shouting at each other in that couple of days, which always ended with her whimpering. She didn't seem like mom any more.

The change in her scared me most when they came to take her away. She struggled and screamed like something from the Circle and she held on tighter to Katy Kay. The men that came had to tear Katy Kay out of mom's arms and then they dragged mom out. I wasn't supposed to see that. Dad had sent us all up to Mrs Kalinsky's two floors up but I'd snuck down because this sudden feeling had chilled me that I needed to see mom. Dad wrestled me back when I tried to stop them taking her and afterwards he told me that it was the drugs that made her act that way. Katy Kay was on the settee turning red with the kind of anger that babies get at being put down unexpectedly. He had to let me go so he could pick her up. By that time, anyway, mom was long gone.

"Scarly, can't you hold on?"

Scarly, in a small voice, answers, "No."

"I want to go too." Sandrine, her twin, still half asleep, always wants to do what Scarly does.

Dad pulls the brakes hard and we all shoot forward. Katy Kay wakes and starts screaming.

"Go in those bushes over there. Hurry up."

Two things I didn't mention about this road. One is that there's nothing on it, no trucks, no cars, no bikes. The other thing is that it's getting dark. Eerie, pale, lemon roadside lights are coming on.

Scarly and Sandrine scramble out of the car and head for the bushes because they're more scared of dad in this mood than of the shadowy roadside.

They're back in when dad turns to us all. "Sorry, kids. Bet it doesn't feel like much of a holiday." He smiles, and in the hard glare of the inside light I think it would have been better for him not to try. "This is what we'll do."

Five pairs of eyes are fixed on him hopefully. Not Katy Kay because she's asleep again. Not me because I have this feeling dad's not being straight with us.

"At the edge of every ring of the Circle there's a frontier hut. You knew that, kids, didn't you?"

No, we didn't know that. The older two are looking more doubtful now.

"The forest hut is just down this road. To be honest with you, I'm completely lost. They're sure to have a map there. They'll get us to Camp Cheer in no time at all."

The ragged chorus of 'OK's doesn't carry much conviction. I think suddenly of mom looking at me as they pulled her through the door, crying out 'Max!' I look at my dad's smiling profile and wonder what's going on. Frontier huts don't sound like something you'd make up even if I haven't heard of them, and surely dad wants to get to Camp Cheer and to safety as badly as we do. I try to believe it as dad switches the engine on again and the road to the forest starts to melt away under the headlights of our jeep.

Kay Kats live in the Ice Pole. They have snowy-white fur and big, shiny eyes. The fur kills at a touch, sending a sharp shock. That's besides its lethal teeth and claws, its super strength. The scarfish live where nothing should be able to survive, in the icy waters of the Sea of Storms. They form a circle round their prey and give a secret signal, seconds after which only ice floes are left, rosy with blood.

Who would make this up? I ask myself question after question as the trees form an army of giants against the indigo sky. I ask myself why there's no sign of light to show us where the frontier hut is. The twins are whimpering. Vern has thankfully fallen asleep. Jackro sits tense beside me. Trixy's holding Katy Kay, still sound asleep, so tight her arms must be aching. We stare at the trees without speaking and the thought comes that I'm desperate to push away that we're never going to find Camp Cheer. I look at the back of dad's head and I feel afraid.

"Dad?" I ask the only question I dare without frightening the others. "Are we near the hut yet?"

I have to repeat it twice before he answers. "The hut?"

"Yeah. The frontier hut. The place they'll have the map."

"Max," he says, slowing the jeep-mobile so he can turn to look at me. "I hate to be doing this."

"Doing what?"

He's turned away, building up speed. We bump up and down in our seats, only the belts holding us down as we hurtle towards the forest.

"I'm so sorry." I hear dad's whisper. I hear the break in his voice. He's crying but he doesn't slow down. "I love you all." I don't think anyone else has heard. They're all crying or screaming.

Suddenly, within yards of the shadow of the trees, he brakes as he did before. He swings out of his door, yanks mine open and pulls me out. "But not this time," he says. "They won't get seven."

I hit the ground, banging my head and my arm twists under me. I cry out in pain and shock. Dad's back in the car. "Run, Max," he says. He slams his door and drives off.

"No!" I yell after him. "Dad! No!"

The jeep-mobile's already racing away, too far in seconds for me to catch it. Run! Why? Where? I stand and watch till the jeep-mobile's swallowed up in the hungry trees. I hear the howling straight away and the cawing of the huge birds that are bombing down from the clear sky into the trees.

"No!" I stand there numb then, as two birds pause mid-flight and turn towards me, I begin to run.

I think maybe these are jacksaw rocs but I'm not hanging around to find out. If they are then maybe there's a truganasau out there somewhere.

I didn't tell you about the truganasau, trug for short. It's all of two storeys of an apartment block high and it's the fiercest of the creatures of the Circle. I'm named Max and first born kids in my class at school have names like mine meaning biggest, first, best. Even the meanest parents aren't going to call their kid Trug. It's the monster I'm named for though. Next to it the other creatures of the Circle are small fry. It lives in the mountains, but at that size and that dangerous, who's going to keep it there? If it exists, of course.

142

If it does exist, it's my creature. If I call it, it's supposed to come. Would it? And would it protect me? Or is what my dad is thinking true? The creatures exist all right but they're out to kill. I remember another version of the story I heard when I was little. A big kid told me, trying to scare me, that the creatures don't protect the ones named for them. They go after them. He said the trug would get me and gobble me up. I heard it later too that it was one way you could get to Galsantos, throw the monsters something to eat and sneak through the Circle one ring at a time. I also heard another version, that the Braga had made some kind of deal with the monsters, sending them sacrifices and that's how they could stay in power. But then you get the complete opposite, saying that the Braga have made the whole thing up.

No-one knows what to think about the Braga anyway. They're a mystery nobody tries to look into unless they want to disappear. No-one's quite sure where they came from or how they suddenly took control of Carthamensas. They've got plenty of money and they've got power, that's for sure. They're a family of a sort, maybe more like a pack, like the vern-wolves.

So, as I run I don't know what to believe. Maybe it's right, there are no monsters. Maybe the birds are just like that out here, defending their territory. Maybe the wolves are howling to warn enemies away. I hope so because one thing I have to believe is that the family's OK, that the jeep-mobile's driving on through the forest. I have to believe that dad's listened to one old wives' tale too many. If the worst has happened, I can't think about that now. I can't go back to find out. I do what dad told me. I run.

I don't think the birds have followed me, but a few seconds ago I thought I heard padding of powerful feet behind me. I thought I heard the panting of a beast moving at speed to kill. I wanted to look back but I didn't. I just ran faster. My head and arm hurt like the pain of the Void. My chest is burning and my legs feel like they're giving out. But I have to keep going. I need to get safe and I need to find mom.

It's getting really dark, which is scary. The road ahead is suddenly lit up and I hear an engine coming close behind. Before I have time to build up hope that it's our jeep-mobile a car pulls up alongside. A worried face, older than my dad, a face I recognize as a well-known member of the Braga Council, peers at me. The car, low and sleek, stops.

"Hey, son, are you OK? Where are you heading? Carthamensas?"

There's no place else. I'm too tired to wonder why he asks. I nod. I'm glad he isn't questioning what I'm doing out running when it's getting dark, in a forbidden place. Perhaps he already knows.

"Hop in. Can you manage that?"

I stumble round to the passenger side and climb in. "I'll run you home," he says. "Where do you live?"

The thought of home, finding our apartment empty, scares me stiff. I'm thinking too is he trying to find out where I live? "Can you just drop me over the border in Carthamensas?"

He gives me a puzzled look. "All right. You sure?"

I'm puzzled too. This is the first time I've been face to face with one of the Braga. He's nothing like I imagined. I wonder if everything I've heard about the Braga is true. I almost feel like opening up to him but maybe this, not all the other things, is the real trap. We drive into town. I'm back. Out of the Outlands, safely away from the Carthamensas Circle.

I don't go near our street. I find an alley, even though I know they're dangerous places after dark. There's no-one about so I risk getting in a big, flip-lid dumpster. The rubbish stinks and there's the danger someone will throw something or someone in, but at least there's a length of plastic, probably a refuse sack for me to lie down on. It's lumpy, with a few sharp things sticking out, but I feel so drowsy that instantly my eyes are closing. I hold on tightly to one thought: find mom. I think too late that I'd have done better to stay in the Outlands to do that. But then I let that thought and all others fall away.

As I feel myself drifting off, my last thoughts are of the forest. I fight sleep to see what the forest has to tell me but it's quiet, very quiet. It's green and dark with the hushed swishing of long branches sweeping the stony, leaf-strewn floor. The branches beat a rhythm of sleep and I'm finding it hard to stay awake a second more. I hope, as the world slips away, that the Carthamensas Circle isn't waiting for me in my dreams.

# The Void

## By David Trebus


My name is Adam. It's a fairly mundane name for what I feel has been a fairly mundane life thus far. Today, however, was different. Today I had the most awful experience of my life, being cast aside by someone dear to me. It felt as if I were disconnected from the flow of life, left by the wayside to watch from a distance. I didn't feel like there was much point in continuing, although my innate fear of the alternative seldom let me ponder anything else.

I took my usual route to work, allowing the same old routine to guide my actions and prevent me having to think. The sky was grey and miserable, reflecting my state of mind. I ended up waiting at the same old crossing at the usual time and stepped out without thinking, too contained within my self-imposed misery to pay attention. I didn't even notice the bus heading towards me. So clichéd, I know.

It was then I found myself in The Void. I didn't so much step into it or walk through some portal, or even just appear here. It somehow felt like I had been here for a very long time without realising it, sitting in a place of absolute nothingness, even when I had been surrounded by the outside world.

If you think that the lack of external stimulus creates a world devoid of passion and life, I would have agreed with you. That was, until I entered the Void. A place of desolation, not cold, not hot, not heavy, not soft, a place just for me, my own personal space with nothing but me inside it. Here I am all that is, all that will be, all that ever was.

But, even with just me here, this place is not what I thought it would be. All I am seems to be laid bare before my eyes in the blackness. I see nothing, yet at the same time I am seeing everything. All the things I have done, my memories. All that I am doing now, existing. All that I will do and hope to do in the future.

I would tell you about my appearance, but in this place it is kind of irrelevant. Before I ended up here, though, if you're curious, I was a tall man in my mid-twenties. I had blond hair, blue eyes and was slimly built. I had an existence: working, hoping, striving for company, surrounded by people, yet curiously alone all the time. That was all before I ended up here, though.

Now I truly am alone, but at the same time I feel like I am with everyone. Being alone implies there are people about to be with in the first place, but here in the Void I am all that ever was, so how could I possibly be alone? My memories speak of past loves, friends, family. They all float with me in my mind. I feel like they are all still here, still with me in my life.

I raise my hand, but there is no light to see it with. So in truth I don't even know if I am moving anything at all. I just perceive the fact I am moving it due to my muscles tensing slightly. I consider this and think about my life before in general. I perceived so many things that I took for granted, but I never considered if my perception of those events was even accurate.

What if I had simply taken another point of view, would that have changed how things had unfolded?

The question burns in my mind, as I struggle to comprehend where I am and who I was. I consider the bad events in my life and how they affected me. I ask myself, if I had looked at them differently, could I have changed things? After all, if it's all down to my perception, then breaking up with a partner could be perceived as the darkest thing in the world or the best possible outcome, leading to a brighter future.

In this world of nothingness, my perceptions and thoughts are the only things that give the Void any reality. The sheer power I seem to wield here feels immense. I begin to realise I have the power to shape the world into anything I want, simply by perceiving it in a different way.

I shut my eyes, substituting darkness for darkness; there is no real change. Just like with raising my hand, I only know I have shut my eyes by the sensation and observance that I have performed the action. Somehow, it still helps me focus as I begin to truly believe in my capability.

I envision the world I once knew, the world I once had at my fingertips, the world I could touch and be a part of by simply reaching out my hand and grasping it. I picture myself in it, as I was, but taller, more confident, stronger. I know my place in the world now, and I know that I have the power to shape it into anything I desire.

I find myself standing back at the crossing on my way to work. I blink, realising that in the single moment it had taken me to make a choice to leave The Void, I had changed my fate for all time. The clouds have all gone, revealing a sunlit afternoon as the bus passes harmlessly before me, and I see my future unfold.

I can feel the world now as I once did. I feel wind on my cheek, through my hair. Sunlight caressing my skin, and air rushing into my lungs as I breath in life. I say goodbye to the Void I once knew, the Void with no light or darkness but simple nothingness, as I pull myself back to what I want.

I smile, knowing that I smile not by inference but by the reactions I perceive around me, feeling that everything is as it should be as I open my eyes.

I open my eyes to the light and look out at the new world full of possibilities.

I look inwards at the light of myself reborn, insight gained into the infinite possibilities that are myself.

## WILLOWS ON THE DARK MERE
## BY NYKI BLATCHLEY

green hair trailing
                        weeping wood
veils the still surface
                        goose haunted
                        mallard mad
in a verdant pavillion
glowering up
                at grey cloud ramparts


gowned in white
broken sword buckled
                                from a hero's hand
the lady points two ways
                        to the future
                        to the past


bramble beset
bog snared
                        the way leads home
                and the lady
still green haired
still sword clad
still exquisite
                        smiles

# Diary of a No-Mark

## By Sandra Norval

**Captain's log stardate: Not sure, some time around 1066 AD**

Landed in a battlefield, bit hair-raising, could've been dangerous. Knocked over some guy, just as an arrow flew by. Lucky it didn't have someone's eye out.

**Captain's log stardate: Not sure, some time around 1666 AD**

Tried to land, was all kicking off. Somehow a fire had started. Got the hell out, updraft blew out the blaze. Didn't even get a thank you.

**Captain's log stardate: Not sure, some time around a few billion years BC**

Couldn't land at all. Bumped into a massive meteor, it went one way, we went the other, screwed up landing for both of us. Took a bit of effort to get back to orbit, time moved on by the time we got back, must've missed the dinosaurs.

**Captain's log stardate: Not sure, some time around 0 BC (ish)**

Took a while to find a safe spot to touch down, had to use main beam for equivalent of a few weeks Earth time. Eventually landed, found everyone had headed off to Bethlehem, guess there's some gig going on. Had to run back to the machine though, bit strange, chased by a dinosaur. Thought they'd gone by now, who'd've thought.

**Captain's log stardate: Not sure, some time around 55 AD**

Starting to think something's up. Saw Romans today, which is about right from what I remember from school. They were dealing with Boodicker (note to self: check spelling). Anyway, that bird that fought back, tough as old boots (wonder if that's where she got her name. Hmm, something to research.)

Shit, err, where was I? Oh, hell, yeah. When I said 'dealing' with her, what I meant to say was, um, feeding her to some Velociraptors. Need to check timelines.

**Captain's log stardate: April 15th, 2117 AD**

Last entry, handing over the machine keys to Admiral Smythe. Half the team wiped out by dinosaur infestation at Base. Turns out it's my fault. Who knew.

# The Festival of Nets

## Part Three: The Catch

### By Sean Patrick Giblin

Demen awoke with a start. His head slammed into a solid bulkhead as he attempted to rise to his feet. Strong, and bright mote-scattered light filtered in from above and all around him. He was in some type of padded cell or pod. Turning, he found that the wall behind him was clear, refracted light shimmered across its smooth surface with rainbow patterns. The glass had become fogged, Demen used one hand to wipe at it and felt a deep relief flooding him when he found that his skin had returned to its normal state of mottled grey and blotchy darkness.

As his hand cleared away the condensation, which he found to be surprisingly cool against his sweaty palm, he stumbled back. Many sets of eyes were watching him. He took a step closer to the glass casing and wiped once more. Outside his small pod stood a collection of men and women in drab, grey medical coats, wooden tablets in hand and some wearing optics.

"Where in the Hags hairy anus am I?" Demen was ashamed at the quavering in his voice. He wasn't sure if it was the strangeness of it all which unnerved him the most or if it was having so many people staring at him at once. He wasn't used to being stared at. He was usually ignored, and that was how he survived.

Another thought crossed his mind, and he frantically searched the room on the opposite side of the glass for the three Reavers who had captured him. Of them he could see no sign. What was this? He'd heard tales of Changelings disappearing without a trace. A place, they said, at the heart of the Horogomy power, where they took children with the curse and experimented on them. He'd heard many wild rumours about such places and about the monstrosities that they created, used to aid the Horogomy in their futile war against the Quarrellrian Empire.

Shit. He was fucked. The Crooked Three had fucked him royally. Had the Weaver been sowing this thread since before his birth? Had the Gamblers luck finally fled him? "Hag curse you all! And fuck all of you!" he screamed, and then he froze as he saw that the people outside were scrawling down notes upon the parchments attached to their wooden tablets. He threw himself at the glass and pounded his fist against it, frantic ripples raging across his skin like the chasing clouds that ran from a storm wind. His display, however, only brought on more frantic motion of moving quills.

After some time he slumped to the floor, exhausted and shaking. He needed his husk; he went to check for it and then remembered he was naked. He thought of his tattered charmer's cloak back in the Narrow Staircases attic room rumpled on the floor and carrying his bag of husk. He thought of the last time he'd been without his husk, it was not something he liked to dwell on, but try as he might he couldn't keep the memories from flooding in.

He was curled on the floor of a sewer, mad with fever as he tried every fungus and spore he could find, hoping that one would contain some trace element of the huskerlyn he needed. He had lain there for days, sweating and gibbering madness. Foam flecked his lips and his body bled from the trails his nails had left in his flesh. The itch was unbearable. Even now he could feel it. It was like maggots crawling beneath the skin. After a while, he would not only start to feel them, but he would also start to hallucinate, seeing his own flesh writhe and move as if thousands of eggs were hatching just beneath that thin surface.

"You're an interesting specimen." a cool, deep voice crooned as if speaking through a thick fog.

A tall, blue-eyed and dark haired man wearing thick optics, hands held behind his back and pristine white lab coat hung open and unbuttoned, stood before him with legs apart. The man raised a hand up to the glass and spread his long fingered and gloved hand wide against it. "Very interesting indeed."

"What the fuck do you want?" Demen spat, hysteria creeping into his voice against his will.

The man ignored him. "Prepare the operating room," he said looking to someone behind him who moved to do his bidding. Then turning back to regard Demen, "And have this one prepped for surgery."

"Surgery? What in the Hag's sagging tits are you fucking talking about? Let me out of here, you fucks. Let me out of here now." Demen beat his fist against the glass. A cloud of gas started to seep its way into the small chamber. He found his breath coming in hard and fast. He beat the glass with all he had, and heard a small crack, but his strength was beginning to waver and leave him completely. His arms flopped to his sides, and his legs gave way beneath him.

There was a hiss and then a pop, or perhaps that was just his own ears, he thought dreamily. The glass slowly shot out and upwards and cool, oddly clean, air rushed into his lungs. Four pairs of arms grabbed him and dragged him upwards, then deposited him on a steel table that made his skin prickle.

He was wheeled down a brightly lit corridor and soon found himself in a circular chamber, a rounded metal table, with strong looking restraints strapped to five points, sat in the middle of the room. On the opposite side of the chamber was a steel desk that contained an assortment of unpleasant-looking instruments, the blue-eyed man stood before this, examining the contents keenly.

"Should we begin Head Researcher?" inquired one of the women who had helped wheel him in.

"Put him on the operating table," the man said, turning as he snapped a thin glove over one hand.

Demen was hoisted up; he tried to struggle, but whatever drug they had given him had done its work good. He couldn't move a muscle other than his eyes and even that felt like trying to push a boulder up a steep hill slick with whale-oil. He was forced back down, and straps were tightened about his ankles, wrists and neck.

The man the woman had called the Head Researcher leaned over him and smiled a smile that never even touched his cold reptilian blue eyes. "Do you know what this is?" he asked, holding up a small, tube-like cylinder made of polished steel and rimmed in bronze.

Demen fought to say something unpleasant about the man's mother but found he was unable to force out any words other than, "mmmfffgggaaammmpppooorrrgggfffff."

"Of course you don't," the man continued to smile down at him. "Otherwise you would have been here before. And trust me; we don't get any who return afterwards." The smile vanished, "prep him!"

More lab coats and hands swirled about his head. Tubes and needles were shoved into his legs, arms, chest, neck and even his cock and balls. Demen now lay there naked and feeling much like a human pin cushion. A buzz of activity moved all around him. He struggled weakly to utter a word and pull free an arm; all the while, a host of unconcerned and uncaring faces moved across his spinning vision. They were all stern men and women, clean shaven, short haired and clean cut. Nobles even, he thought. So not your every day, regular bone cutters either.

Once they had finished whatever the fuck it was they were doing, the table he was on began to revolve and then slide upwards, until he was almost looking back down at the floor. Someone stepped in front of him and he felt something cool being slathered across his head. He moved his eyes and saw the Head Researcher walk towards him from his grisly table of toys, carrying a bonesaw.

Now he felt it. What he had felt before had been nothing like it. He'd been partially indifferent and unconcerned. What could they possibly do to him that was worse than what the Reavers would have done? Now he found himself envying the crippled thief. True, raw panic flared inside him. His eyes bulged out of his skull, and dribble splattered against the green tiled floor beneath him. He wanted to beg and plead with them. Anything to get him out of this nightmare.

Two polished boots clacked in front of him, and he felt fingers tracing across his scalp and the kiss of steel against the back of his head. He thought he closed his eyes as darkness settled upon him and knew that he soiled himself, and then braced himself to meet the Hag in her horrid garden.

There was a grunt and someone cried out and must have stumbled away as instruments fell to the floor in a wild clattering of steel on stone. Demen tried to open his eyes but found that he had never shut them. The lights had gone out. Bodies were dropping all around him, judging by the sound of heavy thumps and grunts. There was the sound of cutting leather. Something hard crashed into him. The floor he guessed. He'd been released from his restraints and then he was tossed over someone's shoulder.

The next few moments were a mix of confusion and bafflement as he saw flickering gas-lights dimming in and out of illumination revealing blood-smeared corridors. At one point he saw a man running towards them carrying a rod of some sort and wearing the regalia of a soldier. Demen's mysterious saviour spun about and, when things righted themselves he caught a brief glance of the soldiers' blood spattered-face, his neck torn open.

This was insane. Had the Hag heard his curses and decided to toss him into a deeper cauldron of shit. First the Reaver's, then those lunatic's in the long coats, and now this stranger who, although seeming small and light of frame, was surprisingly strong. If they could fight soldiers and carry his limp form at the same time, then they must possess even greater talents than he himself did. But where were they taking him?

They came to a darkly lit corridor that had a dead end and a shit trap. Demen had already predicted what was about to happen and braced himself as he was flung down the waste disposal. He slid and flopped his way down the chute, finally being deposited into the murky green waters of the Dryas, the sea that hugged the coast around the bay of Salt Breeze.

The stranger hauled him back up and Demen felt a little lucidity coming back into his body, enough that he could keep his head above water with only limited aid from the stranger. His saviour, or captor, (he hadn't quite figured out which yet,) helped him slide up onto a sludgy bank of marshy green and brown shrubs. He was then tossed a cloak, which he wrapped about himself with zeal. They sat there for a time, neither saying anything, as the pale purpling sun rose over the city. Dawn, he thought, absently.

Demen was about to say something, he wasn't sure what exactly, when a boat came about a corner of a small rocky island and headed straight towards them. He was on his feet instantly and made to run before a hand caught the edge of his cloak. "They're friends," the stranger assured him. He found he still couldn't tell if the voice emanating from the hood was male or female. It was rich and dark, with a slurring quality and a touch of iron command to it.

"Are they now? And what are you?" Demen spat.

The stranger just shrugged.

As the boat neared, he saw that it was a sleek and narrow wavecatcher of Sataran quality and the crew were Sataran too. They even had a Basesk with them, the equivalent to a Changeling on the Sataran islands. The Basesk was covered in tattoos, piercings and bracelets and sat hunched and bored in the stern.

As the wavecatcher slid up the small marshy bank, a sailor leapt off, and braced one foot against the boat and used a barge pole to steady the incoming vessel and ready it for quick re-departure back out to sea.

"Come on you goat fuck get aboard, quickly," the, supposed, captain shouted to Demen.

He did as the man said and found that the stranger did not follow. "You not coming?"

The hooded head shook once. He found it odd that this whole time the stranger had managed to keep that hood up obscuring the features beneath. Try as he might, Demen could not pierce the gloom within. As the wavecatcher made to depart once more, the stranger held out a hand. "Here. For our employer."

The hand held out a familiar cylinder, rimmed in bronze. Demen took it with a frustrated sigh, feeling as though he had been royally played like a mouse in a game of Catcher and Net. As he took the cylinder, he caught a quick flash of bone from beneath the stranger's folds. Then the vessel pulled away from the bank and took to the open waters.

"And this," the stranger shouted and tossed him a small bag as the sleek craft began to drift back out to sea.

He opened the bag to find it contained a dose of hash and husk. He managed to scrounge a pipe from one of the sailors and lit up, savouring the taste of the sweet smoke as it plunged down into his lungs. The harbour bells began to clanger and chime and when he looked back to shore, the stranger was gone. He stared down at the other object in his hand and briefly wondered if any other children of the Fisher had been so lucky to escape the festival with their prizes or lives this night.

He looked at the slowly glittering tiles of the rooftops of Salt Breeze and thought of his attic room and about the tales they would tell of the charm seller who mysteriously disappeared during the night of Nets, leaving all his clothes and wares behind. A small snort escaped him at that, blowing smoke from his nostrils like a bellows. He looked up into the sky and saw the looming dark of the Watcher moon still hanging in its suspended position in the northern sky. Of the Fisher there was no sign.

The Festival of Nets was over for another year. And he'd survived it. Somehow. He knew that there was a catch somewhere in all this, but for the moment he was struggling to find it. He lay back and let the waves and the smoke take over.

# Biographies

## David Trebus

David Trebus is a 30 year old writer based in Hertfordshire. A huge lover of sci-fi, fantasy and Manga, David has always been inspired and loved writing. He especially loves writing stories set in the modern world with a supernatural or sci-fi twist, along with more fantasy themed tales. David currently has a novel published called Guardian Angel, along with his latest comic: Nemhain.

You can find more information on his work and currently released books at www.facebook.com/Dtstories

or his comic page on www.facebook.com/Nemhain

## Nyki Blatchley

Nyki Blatchley is an author, poet and freelance copywriter who graduated from Keele University in English and Greek and now lives in Hoddesdon, Hertfordshire. He's had about forty stories published, mostly fantasy or horror, in various magazines, webzines and anthologies, including Penumbra, Lore, Wily Writers and The

Thirteenth Fontana Book of Great Horror Stories. His novel At An Uncertain Hour was published by StoneGarden, and he's had novellas out from Musa Publishing and Fox & Raven, among others. He's currently working on a fantasy trilogy called The Winter Legend.

Nyki is an administrator for the online fantasy writers' group fantasy-writers.org. He has also had many poems published, and has performed poetry and music at various venues around London, including frequent appearances at the legendary coffee-house Bunjies, which in the 60s hosted artists such as Bob Dylan, Paul Simon and David Bowie.

For more information on Nyki and his writing, please visit http://www.nykiblatchley.co.uk/

and read his blog on http://nyki-blatchley.blogspot.com/

## Lynette Bishop

Lynette Bishop is a retired TEFL teacher, living in Ware, Hertfordshire. She is currently writing a YA fantasy trilogy, Imaginations, set in two worlds. In our world, some of the settings reflect parts of her life. London is where her son Tim lives. Second son, Chris was in Madrid for several years. Daughter, Becky lives with her Italian husband and two sons in Florence. Central to the action is Prague where Lynette lived for three years. The other world, Tresarios reflects a fascination in our mysterious universe. She knows nobody who actually lives there.

Previous books in the same genre, but simpler, are for a younger age range of 8 to 14 year olds. Three of the four books, written for Scripture Union in the '80s and early '90s, can be found on Amazon: Escape from Gehalla, The Key of Zorgen and Race to Anderloss.

Finally, there are some short stories, all set in cafes. The first two are published in Encounters, the anthology of another writers' group, Hertford Writers' Circle. Ten stories have followed since, and some of them may end up in magazines. They are not specifically fantasy but a mix of genres, and none of them are like the story which won a competition in Woman's Realm in 1997. Cafes are where Lynette finds it easiest to write and she dreams of producing a book of cafe stories which can be actually read in cafes while sipping a latte.

She hopes you will dream your own dreams along with her as you read the stories she has written for this book. They are not set in cafes. Far from it...

## Sean Patrick Giblin

Sean Patrick Giblin is a 30 year old writer from London. He has spent the last eight years crafting both his writing style and his world, planning out a series of four trilogies that will make up the Legacies Saga. The short story, the Festival of Nets, is a story from this world. He has also been working on another project called The Pantheon, of which the first book Blood Calls Blood is already finished. Sean spent much of his early twenties touring in a band and living in Japan. He has now embarked on a new adventure to travel the states and live in Canada, where he, in the words of Bilbo Baggins, can see some mountains and find somewhere peaceful, where he can finish his book, or book's as in his case.

To contact Sean, send an email to seanpatrickgiblin@fsmail.net

## Sandra Norval

Sandra Norval is an environmentalist by day but her alter ego loves to work on horror, fantasy and sci-fi when she's not looking. Ranging from angels and demons to fairies and alternative realities her tales are inspired by her dreams and nightmares - why wouldn't she share them with you? When not writing fiction she also writes articles and research papers on environmental issues.

You can find Sandra at sandranorval.wordpress.com or on twitter @sandranorval'

www.ingramcontent.com/pod-product-compliance
Lightning Source LLC
Chambersburg PA
CBHW072150170626
46813CB00004BA/1745